THE BROKEN BRIDGE

A SUCCULENT SLEUTH COZY MYSTERY

IRIS MARCH

ALSO BY IRIS MARCH

The Story That Made Us Stronger

The Succulent Sleuth Cozy Mystery Series

Terra Cotta Theft – prequel short story, newsletter reader exclusive

The Library Attic Attack – second story in the series, short story also contained within A Bookworm of a Suspect anthology

More coming soon...

The Broken Bridge: A Succulent Sleuth Cozy Mystery

Copyright © 2022 Iris March

Cover design by Mallory Rock of Rock Solid Book Design (www.RockSolidBookDesign.com)

All rights reserved. No part of this book may be reproduced or used in any manner without the written permission of the copyright owner except for the use of quotations in a book review.

This story is a work of fiction. Names, characters, places, and incidents are the product of the author's imagination or are used fictitiously. Any resemblance to actual persons, living or dead, or events is entirely coincidental.

The Buckeye Trail, the Buckeye Trail Association, The Ohio State University, Ohio University, and the Ohio State University Agricultural Technical Institute are all real institutions but are used in this book fictitiously.

Wandering Gingko Press

Ebook ISBN: 979-8-9859182-0-5

Paperback ISBN: 979-8-9859182-1-2

Dedicated to my sweet nieces and nephews, especially Molly

PROLOGUE

It had rained the night before, so the Buckeye Trail was soft. Brooks ran this stretch of trail regularly and knew where the puddles would be and which roots would be especially slippery, making them dangerous. He often ran after work, which helped him mentally divide his time at home from time at the office. Running had always been a blissful stress reliever for him and now was also a way to drown out sorrow. He listened to fast-paced rock music to help him keep a quick, steady cadence.

On this particular day, Brooks was running out and back on the same section of trail. Sometimes he asked a coworker to drop him off at one trailhead and parked his car at another to make a straight run. Today, Brooks looked forward to the waterfall that he'd get to see twice.

Brooks pushed himself to try to beat his normal

time for this route. He didn't expect to run faster than he ever had before.

Brooks ran hard on the first leg of his run. He was satisfied with his time and took it easy as he turned around and ran back toward his car. Within the second mile, right after the waterfall, he noticed something different. Brooks spotted a red backpack on the edge of the trail, behind a tree without its owner in view. Was it abandoned? He had not seen anyone else since he passed this spot the first time. He considered that perhaps a hiker was "using the facilities" farther off the trail and put the pack out of his head. Brooks let his mind wander and looked up at the leaves moving in the breeze. He noticed that the shadows of oak leaves were slightly different from those of maple tree leaves. Nature was such a wonderful healer.

When he turned his attention back to the trail, Brooks spied a polished walking stick just off the trail. It was broken into two jagged pieces and had definitely not been there when he ran past that spot not even a half hour ago. He stopped and picked up the longer piece, inspecting the smooth, glossy wood. He looked around and searched for another person within the forest. Again, there was no one around. What could he do to respond to this discovery? Who would he report this to? Why was it broken? Brooks' heart rate was already up from exercising, but he felt like someone was watching him

The Broken Bridge

and he itched to move on. Had anyone been there, he would have stopped to help them, but now he left the walking stick and ran on, wondering what actions to take.

Near the end of the trail, Brooks found himself on the familiar truss bridge over the river. He'd always loved the noise that his feet made as they pounded the wood mixed with the river's happy gurgling. *Thwomp thwomp thwomp.* His eyes were on the water: the swirls of the eddies and riffles were mesmerizing. But halfway across the bridge, Brooks stopped in his tracks. The bridge supports were cracked. Part of the railing was broken clear through. And there were splatters of wet blood on the trusses. The bridge had been whole and clean when he had plowed past that exact location, arms pumping hard. He turned around, looking for someone else, anyone. What happened here? Were the abandoned pack and the walking stick related to the damage and this grisly scene? Brooks jogged to the end of the bridge to get away from the gore and immediately called the authorities.

"Nine-one-one. What's your emergency? This is Stacey," a woman said on the other end of the line.

"My name is Brooks Thompson. I'm on the Buckeye Trail in Hawthorn Heights, and the bridge over the river is broken and there's some fresh blood." He stopped speaking for a moment because he couldn't catch his breath. "I found a backpack and a broken walking stick abandoned farther up the trail. Someone is in trouble, I think."

"Are you in danger, sir?" she asked.

Brooks looked around and saw only trees and underbrush. Birds chirped. It was a sunny, pleasant afternoon. "I don't think so."

"We can send a police unit to the scene. Tell me your location."

"I can meet the police at the Buckeye Trail trailhead off of Main Street," he said.

"Can you tell me your precise location, sir?"

"Uh, I don't know the address for the trail." Brooks didn't know how to tell the dispatcher where he was. "I'll just meet them at the garden center. Patty's Plant Place. The parking lot is connected to the parking lot for the trail. It's also on Main Street."

"I'll send a unit right away."

And then Brooks finished his run faster than he expected, faster than he had ever run that route. He ran away from the violence that happened and toward the help he could provide.

1

A SCHOOL BUS AND PINK CONEFLOWERS

As Molly Green checked out one of her regular customers, she heard the bell over the door jingle and looked up. The customer, Harriett, was buying yet another bottle of Molly's strong-smelling vinegar-based weed killer along with her third flat of petunias that week.

"I really think these purple ladies will fill out the space finally," the short older woman told Molly. Harriett always referred to flowers as "ladies," and Molly loved to play along during their conversations.

Molly gave her regular sales pitch as she watched a hiker enter the garden center out of the corner of her eye. "I bet they will. You must really be packing these girls in. Remember, we're selling milkweed at our cost for the month of June to encourage more plantings."

"You know I'll be back soon, Molly," Harriett said

as she handed over her credit card. "I'm still holding out for the milkweed seeds that I planted last fall. We'll see if they come up. I want to do my part for the monarchs. You know I do." Molly nodded. They had certainly had the full conversation before about how milkweed leaves are the butterfly's only food source after they emerge from the chrysalis. They shared concern over the species' dwindling numbers.

As the credit card machine worked, Molly watched the hiker who had just entered. He looked to be in his early twenties and wore a navy-blue handkerchief as a headband, carried a polished walking stick, and had a hefty red pack on his back. No doubt he had been hiking the Buckeye Trail that ran behind the garden center's property and needed to use the bathroom. She made eye contact while she waited for the machine to do its thing.

"You can just leave your pack here," she called to him, pointing. "Bathroom is right around the corner."

He shuffled over, avoiding a display of gardening gloves of various floral patterns, and let his bag fall to the floor. He mumbled, "Appreciate it," before making a beeline to the bathroom.

Harriett said her farewells, and Molly tidied up the counter. She put the pen Harriett had used back into the pen corral and wiped off some soil with a rag she kept handy for that purpose.

After the hiker emerged from his pit stop, Molly

greeted him properly. "Welcome to Patty's Plant Place. Thanks for stopping in. We have some snacks and chilled drinks in the corner for hikers. Long-term hikers often need more snacks than they expected." This was a standard, practiced line she gave Buckeye Trail hikers who visited the shop.

"Yeah, I'm totally hungrier than I thought I'd be. My name is Trevor. Are you Patty?" he asked, extending his hand.

"I'm Molly. My grandma was Patty. She used to own the place. Nice to meet you." Molly shook his hand, used to being asked if she was Patty. "How far are you hiking the trail?"

"I'm hoping to make the whole loop," he told her enthusiastically. "I just started three days ago. It's been so great being in the woods all day and camping every night. I'm hoping to make it to a bed and breakfast tomorrow so I can take a proper shower."

"What a wonderful summer break. Most people usually just hike for a weekend or a week. They'll do the complete 1,444-mile circuit through Ohio over a few years."

"Well, I'll be a senior at Ohio University next fall," he said. "You know, in southern Ohio. I figured I should do something cool like this before I need to figure out the whole real world job thing. I'm getting over a pretty bad breakup too. You know how it goes.

A major change of scenery is good for that type of thing." He shrugged and looked away.

"Nature has a way of healing hearts, for sure. And jobs get in the way of hiking for weeks at a time. This will be a great start of the summer for you."

"Totally," Trevor smiled, his sheepishness gone. "I've got an internship lined up for the month before I get back to school. Environmental engineering major."

She nodded. "Sounds great. As I said, we've got some granola bars, trail mix, chips, and drinks on that shelf." The way he was eyeing the food corner, she could tell he was itching to take a look, so she stepped aside. She had never been great at small talk with shop newcomers, anyway.

"Thanks," he said and headed for the snacks.

Molly ducked into the back room to find her twin sister, May Flores-Sato, printing out a flower order on the back of an order from last week to conserve trees used to make paper. Molly used her knowledge of flowers to handle the programming side of their operation, while May took care of financials, sales, and marketing.

Besides May, Sherlock, the garden center cat, was also sitting at their computer station. He was staring at the printer paper slowly exiting the printer, ready to attack it. Sherlock was a short-haired black-and-white tuxedo cat who regularly greeted customers and basked in the sunshine or on bags of mulch or pea gravel warmed by the sun. Although he was an outside cat who could go wherever he pleased, Sherlock generally spent the night in the shop and ate the kitty kibble they left out. Molly considered him part of the staff.

May stood up from the computer station, beaming. "We've got another succulent add-on. I'm telling you, these little succulents are really increasing profits. We've sold twice as many living arrangements as we did last quarter so far. People love them."

"Not another succulent," Molly replied, slumping where she stood. "They're killing me. I can only do so much with those things." This was their regular relationship cadence: Where Molly wore her brown hair short, almost in a pixie cut, May's matching brown hair fell down her back. Molly loved colorful, patterned clothing, and May wore muted tones and solids. May was chatty; Molly was quiet. May always wanted to bring order and loved the black and white of numbers, while Molly was drawn to the colors, textures, and tones of flowers. They were opposites: identical twins with very different tastes and opinions.

"No one would know if you just copied the same arrangement all the time. They're all going to different customers. You don't have to get that creative." May poked Molly's arm, handing over the paper. Molly knew she was probably being a little dramatic, but still.

"A sale is a sale," Molly and May both said at the same time, but with different inflections. Smiles plastered their matching faces, and they both rolled their eyes, chuckling. They jinxed each other nearly every day.

"Do you want to check out the hiker buying snacks so I can get started? When is the delivery?" Molly scanned the order page. Sherlock abandoned his paper hunt and wandered into the front of the store.

"You've got until tomorrow afternoon to come up with something new and magical to include three succulents, your signature lame twigs, and something purple. I'll go ring up the hiker." May poked her again and stepped onto the sales floor. With a clipboard in hand—that actually belonged to May—Molly wandered into the adjoining staff greenhouse to assess whether she needed to place an order to include "something purple." She decided that they had plenty of succulents with purple tones and annuals that would match.

Molly went back out to the sales floor to find Trevor chatting with Theo about the waterfall up the trail. He didn't seem ready to check out any time soon. Theo Alexopoulos was one of three full-time employees and was in their local semi-pro soccer league. He did most of the actual heavy lifting and forklift work, including hauling bags of potting soil, mulch, and flats of flowers into the trunks of adoring women. Molly thought the ladies were attracted to his black curly hair that fell below his ears. He was also extroverted, intensely friendly, and quite the show-off with the forklift, zooming around as though he were on the soccer field.

Less than ten minutes later, a school bus delivered May's kids to the parking lot. Hannah and Noah burst into the store, backpacks and arms loaded with projects they were taking home at the end of the school year. Molly was especially excited to see bean sprouts grown in cups.

"Yay! Second to last day of school—done!" May cheered with her arms raised, turning in circles. The kids cheered and danced around her in response, and then both gave her a hug at the same time. While Molly was admiring her twin's supermom powers, she received her own double hug from her niece and nephew.

May supplied the kids with snacks while Trevor gave himself a self-guided tour of the greenhouse. When he returned to the counter, Trevor made jokes that Hannah and Noah ate up. "Where did the king keep his armies?" he asked them.

"In his castle, right? Where else?" Noah asked, munching a cinnamon graham cracker.

"In his sleevies!" Trevor said, tugging on the sleeve of his T-shirt. Molly and May both groaned, but the kids and Theo laughed. Sherlock headbutted Trevor's arm to tell him he didn't care about jokes and that Trevor needed to keep scratching behind his ears.

Molly rang up more customers. May and her children were packing up to leave and Molly was finally checking Trevor out when Theo called out a loud but bored "Hey-o." Molly knew the jovial atmosphere was about to disappear.

"Hey-o," Molly, May, Noah, and Hannah all called back at the same time without looking up.

"Are you guys yodeling in unison now?" Trevor asked, laughing.

"That's our quick way of letting each other know our cousin is about to arrive," Molly told him with a grin. "And Theo really gets a kick out of saying stuff in unison. May and I jinx each other significantly more often than most people do, and it can get kind of weird for him."

As Trevor stowed his snacks in his bag, Shannon Flores entered the store in all her glory. Her fitted gray skirt suit, perfectly adjusted pink summer scarf, and bright pink lipstick screamed "I own this place," and, sadly, she did. Actually, she owned a third of it. The three cousins had inherited the shop from their Grandma and Grandpa Flores six years ago.

"Hi, Shannon. We're just leaving for the day. See you around," May told her, ushering the kids out the door in a rush. May avoided Shannon as much as possible.

"Good to see you too," Shannon responded

absently, patting Hannah on the head without looking at her. Hannah pretended to wipe off her glossy black hair, but Shannon didn't notice. Perching her sunglasses on top of her head, Shannon moved farther into the shop, looking for Molly, and the trio left. Shannon's brown wedge bob swayed as she looked around. Trevor waved at Molly and took his leave as well.

Molly had never understood why Shannon needed to physically visit the garden center, other than the power trip it obviously gave her. Every week, Molly sent her detailed emails with expenditures, profits, losses, and all the data that Shannon would really want to see. Of course, May actually did the math for the report, but Molly was the messenger.

Molly heard the back door chime and assumed Theo had gone to the back lot, where all the trees and flats were displayed under pergolas. He, too, avoided Shannon as best he could. And so Molly was alone with her cousin. She took a deep breath and walked around the counter to face Shannon.

"Seems dead in here today," Shannon pouted, looking around. She held her designer leather purse on her elbow, her hand limp.

Molly ignored the comment and just said, "Hey, how's it going?"

Shannon finally looked at Molly. "I need some flowers to give to my boss. He's finally announced that he's retiring. I want to be the first one to present a gift." Shannon worked in commercial real estate and was always angling to get to the top of her small corporate ladder.

"Well, we sure have flowers here, but a potted plant will last a lot longer than a bouquet in a vase. Or would you like something that he could plant in his garden? Does he have a garden?"

"I want something that will remind him of me for a while," Shannon agreed, still without smiling. "A garden plant sounds good."

"What about a native plant that he won't have to water a lot? You know, already suited to our climate? Purple coneflowers are actually pink and get really tall," Molly said thoughtfully, while considering other plants in her head that Shannon would like.

"I don't know what that is. But pink, you say?" Shannon asked, fiddling with her rose-gold hoop earrings. Looking at Shannon's ears, Molly noticed that Shannon's neck above her scarf and her forehead were sweaty. It certainly wasn't like Shannon to work up a sweat from just walking into the shop from her leather-padded and highly air-conditioned Lexus SUV.

Molly blinked. "They're bright pink and they attract butterflies and other pollinators. Coneflowers are really easy to care for and can grow up to five feet tall. I could wrap up the plastic pot with some fancy fabric, or we could find a cool pot, if you want."

"Big and pink sounds like it would remind him of me. Let's have a look." And so Molly led Shannon to the back lot to select a potted plant. Out of the corner of her eye, she saw Theo duck behind the larger trees they had for sale to avoid her cousin. She was glad that Shannon didn't come demanding program changes or a rearrangement of the store. Molly had had to change Shannon's mind about these types of things more than once. Thankfully, Shannon seemed happy with the selection of coneflowers and her purchase.

2
A BACKPACK AND AN EDITOR

Charlotte, one of the high school students that helped in the evenings and weekends, practically skipped into the shop to start her shift at 4:00 p.m. Charlotte had the longest white-blonde hair that Molly had ever seen in her life. The young lady often wore it in elaborate braids that wound around her head. Molly hoped that one day she'd braid her own daughter's hair in such a way, but didn't have any children yet. Charlotte held state championship records for the sixteen-hundred-meter race, basically a one-mile sprint around the track. Molly guessed that Charlotte was happy to be at the shop because it seemed that she and Ryan, another high school worker, were becoming a bit of an item. Ryan was not in any sports that Molly was aware of, but he was quite the artist. He was a painter, despite being born with only a thumb on his left hand, no fingers at all. It never slowed him down, and Molly usually forgot about this difference.

In general, the evening shifts at the garden center were left to the high schoolers, but one or two evenings a month, Molly or Theo would come in late and stay with them to be sure things ran smoothly. May, Theo, and Molly all took turns on Saturdays if the students couldn't cover their shifts. The shop was closed on Sundays. Grandma Patty and Grandpa Will had always closed on Sundays and major holidays—and Molly and May had been able to convince Shannon to keep it that way so far.

Molly was in cleanup mode before leaving for the day at four thirty. As she adjusted a display of lilies, she got a text from Archie Wilson.

"Checked into my hotel an hour ago. Want to get on that trail before dinner!"

Besides managing the garden center, Molly contributed feature articles to *Gardening Tomorrow*, a monthly magazine. Archie was the editor in chief and would be in the area for the weekend because of the local Home and Garden Show. She and Archie had not met in person yet and had agreed to get together while he was in town. She wasn't sure how to respond. Did he want her to show him the trail? He probably meant the Buckeye Trail, but she didn't remember ever emailing him about it.

"What's up?" Theo asked, waving his hand in

front of Molly's face. "You're frowning, and it's time for you to jet."

"I guess I was thinking too hard. Remember how I told you my editor was going to be around this weekend? He's here, but I don't know if he wants to meet up yet."

"Well, do you want to meet up? Isn't Thursday always Claudia - and - Molly - braid - each - other's - hair - night, or something else way too girly for a totally manly guy like me to care about?"

"Theo!" Molly laughed, punching him on the arm. "You're right. Claudia and I are doing our normal drinks-and-desserts night. No hair braiding! So, not a good night to meet Archie." She absently bent down to pet Sherlock's head, who readjusted himself so that she could also pet his back and tail.

"So, get outta here," Theo said. Molly did need to get home to have dinner with her husband, Scott, before meeting Claudia, who had been her best friend since middle school. Molly laughed again and headed to the staff area to collect her bag and jacket. The display was fine as it was, she told herself. Sherlock bounded in front of her, leading the way.

As Molly reached the backroom doorway, a runner slammed the front door open, and doubled over, hands on his knees, breathing hard.

"Dude! Are you okay?" Theo was at the runner's side before Molly could even turn around.

"I'm. Meeting. The police. Here," the man announced between labored breaths.

"Police?" Charlotte asked, eyes panicky.

"I think. Someone was hurt. On the trail," the man said, standing up to his full height. Molly got a bottle of water from the glass-front fridge and hurried over to hand it to the runner.

"Oh, man. What happened?" Theo asked. Charlotte came out from behind the counter, arms crossed.

"Thanks," the runner said to Molly with a nod and took a swig. "I sprinted here after I called the police. I found a backpack and a walking stick. The stick was snapped in half. The backpack was off the trail, hidden behind a tree. It seemed fishy. But then I got to the bridge over the river."

The garden center crew all nodded. "We know the bridge," Theo told him, looking at Molly. All she could see in her mind's eye was happy, friendly Trevor.

"The wooden guardrail over the bridge? It's broken."

"Oh, no!" Charlotte covered her mouth with her hands and Molly got goosebumps. *Trevor!*

"And the thing is, I ran an out-and-back course today. It wasn't broken when I ran past it the first time."

Molly could hear sirens in the distance, and they all cocked their heads. Molly rubbed her arms. A few seconds went by without movement or conversation. The trailhead was just across the garden center's large parking lot, and it often served as an overflow lot for weekend hikers. It made sense for the police to meet the runner there.

"You should sit down," Theo announced, and retrieved a stool from behind the counter.

"Thanks," the runner mumbled, "but I should stretch." He put his water bottle on the stool and put his hands on his hips to start a squatting quadriceps stretch.

The front door chimed, and they all looked up. Molly was expecting the police, but instead, it was a tall, dark-haired man. He was wearing barely worn but muddy hiking boots and a gray button-up shirt.

"Molly?" he said, looking at her face and then her magnetic name tag. "Hey, it's Archie. Am I interrupting something? What's with all the police outside?"

3

POLICE AND LUNCH PLANS

Brooks Thompson, the runner, was still in the parking lot answering questions for the police. The Patty's Plant Place staff had already provided what they knew about Trevor. Each of them had given a statement individually. A team of police had followed the trail to document the scene. Molly saw out the garden center's side window that one policeman had just returned with the backpack and two pieces of a broken walking stick. Even from that distance, Molly knew they were Trevor's.

Molly, Theo, and Charlotte were all leaning on the counter, each mired in their own thoughts. Archie stood next to Molly but had said little after he figured out what was going on, though he was active on his phone. On the counter, Sherlock sat dutifully at attention next to his people. He headbutted each employee in turn and was rewarded with the lavish affection he expected.

Molly texted Scott again, telling him she wasn't sure when she'd be home. She knew he'd be hungry, but he would want to wait to eat with her. His mind was usually on his next meal. Molly had already called May and told her what was happening. She wondered if she should also let Shannon know, but wasn't sure if this crime would really affect business. It wasn't as if Thursday nights were always booming. She was thinking of texting Claudia, too. It looked like their desserts-and-drinks night might start later than expected.

The bell chimed when Officer Owen came in with the red pack and walking stick fragments. He was the bespectacled policeman who had taken Molly's statement a bit earlier.

"Take a look at these items, please. Do you recognize them?" Owen asked, holding up the gear. A policewoman entered the shop behind him. Her dark red hair was a stark contrast to her standard navy-blue police hat. Molly fleetingly wondered if she had kids who had matching red locks.

Molly nodded an affirmative and felt tears welling in her eyes for the first time. Charlotte watched closely, hugging herself.

"Yeah, yeah. They are his," Theo confirmed, looking at the floor.

"They belonged to the young man," Officer Owen told the ginger policewoman, as if she hadn't heard it herself.

"I was afraid of that," Owen continued, addressing the Patty's Plant Place staff. "We will take them back to the precinct to document the contents of the backpack and place them in the evidence locker. We were able to lift a name with just a little digging, and it was obvious he had just visited your shop. Trail mix right on top." Owen placed the backpack on the counter and adjusted his glasses. Molly wiped away tears thinking of Trevor's purchase. Officer Owen scribbled in his notebook and said something to the policewoman that Molly didn't hear.

She stepped away from the counter and took a deep breath, looking away from the bag and broken walking stick and through the window. Outside, uniformed officers stretched police tape along the entrance to the trail toward the bridge as if it were a Christmas tree garland. Archie followed Molly away from the action.

"This sure is an eventful afternoon. Quite honestly, this is not how I thought I would have met you for the first time," Archie said. She nodded, collecting herself.

"It's nice to finally meet you in person. I'm glad you're in town," she said.

"I really did want to go for a hike on the Buckeye Trail before spending all weekend at the Home and Garden Show. It's nice to be outside in the fresh air before being cooped up and indoors with so many people. These sorts of events are held in large spaces but can still feel confining."

"Well, I guess you could go the other direction, if you really wanted?" Molly suggested without enthusiasm.

"Seems like ill timing to be out on the trail when a young man has gone missing." Archie paused and then asked, "Are you planning on attending the show at all this weekend? I could really use some help scouting out products and companies that we want to pursue. I meant to ask you earlier." Molly suspected that he had not just thought of this invitation off the top of his head.

"Oh, well, I'm not really sure. I couldn't on Saturday." She turned and looked at Theo. He had obviously been listening to the conversation, and he shrugged. "I'll have to see how busy the shop is tomorrow."

Theo stepped closer and said, "I'm sure you can get away for a couple of hours. You leave to make deliveries a few times a week. May and I can handle it."

"Okay. Then, sure, I'd love to go," Molly smiled for the first time since Brooks had come into the shop.

"Great! We should have lunch together, too, to discuss our findings at the show," Archie said. "There's a cool little place just a few blocks down the street that I've been to before that I'm sure you'll love. Let me know when you're at the convention center, and I'll meet you at the door to give you your ticket. They always give us more tickets than we really need for free, but you have to show that physical ticket to get in." Archie was smiling, his eyes big. It was the most he had said the entire afternoon, and Molly wasn't quite sure how to react. He had a lot to say.

"Great," Molly said, but she couldn't bring herself to match his energy.

With that, Archie left Molly's side and asked the police if it would be alright for him to leave. The policewoman double-checked that they had his contact information, and he departed. As the doorbell jingled, Molly felt a bit of a weight lift, as if she had been trying to keep herself more together to put on a professional front with her editor. She made eye contact with Theo, who came over and put his arms around her shoulders. Grateful, she leaned into the hug.

Charlotte joined the group hug, and Molly saw Officer Owen give them a sideways glance. She didn't care what he thought. Her garden center people shared all the love and emotion she was feeling.

A few minutes later, Molly made a call that she knew Shannon would not agree with. "Let's close up shop for the night, Charlotte. I'll call Ryan and tell him not to come in. Go home and hug your doggies." The police officers left the shop a few minutes later, but remained in the parking lot for another half hour. Brooks left shortly after Charlotte. Both Molly and Theo left after the police did.

4

DRINKS AND DESSERTS PLUS TWO

While driving to her favorite bistro in Hawthorn Heights, unfortunately named the Scottish Ferret, Molly told Claudia over the phone, "His cell phone wasn't in the pack, so they didn't have his emergency contact information. He had written his name on the inside of a notebook, though: Trevor Collins."

"Trevor Collins. I bet he's a sweet boy," Claudia tsked.

"I told the police that he said he went to Ohio University, so I'm sure they'll figure out who he was. Can you imagine? His parents don't even know yet. They'll be so worried when they find out he's missing and without his gear."

"Oh, his poor parents. But look at you helping the detectives."

"I'm not sure they were detectives, just police officers. But we were the last people he talked to, Claud. I almost feel responsible somehow."

"Molly, you are so not responsible for whatever happened to that boy, and you know it. You had nothing to do with it." Claudia's firm tone and decisiveness often had a way of shutting down Molly's worry.

"I just feel really connected to it all. It's so horrible and I'm so worried about him." She paused for a beat as she turned into the parking lot. "I'm pulling in now, and I see Scott. You'll be here in a few?"

"Yep, we're almost there."

Molly had agreed with Scott that their late dinner should become a night out with both Claudia and Scott instead of Molly's separate dinner at home and dessert plans at the restaurant. At the last minute, Claudia invited her new boyfriend, Craig. Molly wasn't sure that this emotionally charged day was the best time to meet someone new, but she was glad Claudia wasn't putting off the introductions any longer. As she drove slowly through the parking lot, looking for an open spot, Molly wiped her sweaty palms on her jeans and turned the steering wheel with one hand, alternating left to right. Claudia had been dating Craig for a month already, but Molly hadn't met him yet. As she pulled into a parking bay,

The Broken Bridge

she let out a long breath, thinking about her friend's past bad luck with relationships. Just under three years ago, Claudia's fiancé had left her days before their wedding, and the most recent man had stolen money from her. Molly hoped Craig had a better moral compass and that the relationship had some staying power.

Scott, always early, was waiting for her. This time, he patiently watched her walk through the parking lot. She could see the worry line between his gray eyes, showing that he, too, was feeling the heaviness of the day. As they embraced, Molly exhaled a deep sigh into his chest, resting her forehead against his end-of-the-day stubble, smelling the familiar spicy scent of his cologne. She felt muscles in her back relax that she hadn't even realized were tense.

Molly's mood shifted further out of despair as she settled into her seat in the Scottish Ferret. The well-known smells of fried food and fresh ground coffee wafted over her. She welcomed the corny plaid wall hangings and little flags at the tables. Molly already knew she'd be ordering the fish tacos, and Scott would act like he'd order something different but would settle on his regular burger with zucchini fries. Claudia would get either soup and salad or the fish tacos too. They'd all split the chocolate dessert of the day and order decaf coffee. Predictability felt good on a day like this one.

Scott was engrossed in the menu when Claudia led Craig to their table.

"Molls!" Claudia said at the same time Molly squealed, "Claud!" Their greeting was always a hard, swaying hug. Scott stood up to shake Craig's hand, and Claudia made formal introductions.

"It's so good to meet you, Craig," Molly told him, making herself smile more than she felt she could.

"I'm happy to be here," he replied. He pulled out Claudia's chair for her and pushed it in. Scott gave an ever-so-slight approving nod to Molly, who returned a tiny nod in reply, with an eyebrow arched. This seemed good.

Craig Murdstone was a lot taller than she'd expected, even when he was sitting down, and had very short brown hair with a thinning spot in the back. He was attractive in his own way, Molly decided.

"Claudia says you just moved here," Scott said. "How do you like the area? You have a place here in Hawthorn Heights?"

"It's great. I am here in town. Been trying to get my rented house in order," Craig replied. "The gardening hasn't been agreeing with me." He raised his right hand, which had a bandage on his knuckle. "I just took a position at the local college as a math professor. This quiet town is the perfect place to prepare for classes before the semester starts." Molly and Scott nodded their agreement.

"Craig has a PhD in applied mathematics from Florida Tech," Claudia boasted. Having no interest in or knowledge of math, Molly found her head was heavier as she continued to nod with less enthusiasm.

"I've been working my way north, it seems," Craig told the table. "I've taught at a few other universities, but I'm really hoping to get tenure here."

Before the conversation continued, Claudia made sure everyone had decided on their food selection. Scott and Molly ordered their usual and expected meals. Molly's mouth was watering for her fish tacos, and her stomach growled. When Claudia and Craig told their young waitress they wanted Cobb salads, Scott and Molly exchanged raised eyebrows, and Molly slightly pursed her lips.

While they waited for their meals, Scott and Craig discovered they were both runners.

"I really love running on the Buckeye Trail," Scott said. "There are a few spots on the trail farther from town that have less gravel with rough spots and I have to slow down. I prefer not to run on dirt or mud, usually. But the trails right behind Patty's Plant Place are great, well maintained."

Craig took a sip of his beer and swallowed before answering. "I'll have to check the trail out. I do like running on trails, but it's nice to just start and end at home in the neighborhood. I haven't found any paved trails nearby yet. Do you know of any?"

"The local Park District has some nice, paved, flat trails on the other side of Hawthorn Heights. They link up to more trail systems too, but nothing goes as far as the Buckeye Trail, which makes a circle within the entire state."

"It's really popular. We get a lot of tourists in town because of the Buckeye Trail," Claudia told Craig.

Molly gave a quiet "Uh-huh" in agreement and then chimed in, "My magazine editor arrived in town today, and it looks like he might have bought new hiking boots just to hike the trail."

"Oh, Archie got here today?" Scott asked, hunching his shoulders a bit. "He's going to the Home and Garden Show for the weekend, right?"

"He actually arrived right before the police. He stayed in the shop for an hour or so once they got there."

"Why did he stay so long?" Scott asked. "I'm surprised they didn't kick him out or something."

"I don't know," Molly responded. "They didn't know who he was right away. I just met him in person today. They wanted all of us to stay to answer questions."

"It's always nice to meet people in the flesh instead of only having virtual relationships," Scott said.

"Craig and I met online," Claudia announced, as

if Molly and Scott didn't know this detail about her relationship.

"Well, Archie always seems a bit too friendly to me, emailing when it's just not needed," Scott said, and then changed the subject to the Cleveland baseball season.

5

A MORNING HIKE AND A SUSPICIOUS EARRING

The next morning, Molly was walking on the Buckeye Trail herself. Scott was running the same trail, much faster and farther ahead. Molly was not at all a runner like Scott but knew the value of time alone in nature, even if it was 6:00 a.m. and she was wearing a headlamp. It was dark in the woods in the mornings, and she didn't want to trip over a rut in the path or a tree root. Scott's headlamp matched the lamp that Molly wore, but his had much more prominent sweat stains.

Neither she nor Scott had slept well the night before. It may have been some of the alcohol from their dinner at the Scottish Ferret, but Molly rarely had a hard time staying asleep after a couple of cocktails. She couldn't get Trevor's face out of her head when she was awake. And when she was asleep, she kept having dreams in which Brooks, the runner, and Archie, the editor, were chatting at the shop. They both were admiring Trevor's walking stick in the dream. She yelled at them to do something, to help find Trevor, but they just continued to discuss the walking stick. She hated that the stick was broken and that, as far as she knew, they had no leads about where he was. They had to find him. Had he been kidnapped? He couldn't be dead; he had to be missing. Unpleasant situations always seemed to be so much more extreme in the middle of the night.

And so the couple had admitted defeat and decided that physical activity would be better than chasing sleep that refused to come in the early morning. Scott said that his conversation with Craig at dinner inspired him to run the trail that day. They drove to the garden center and took the trail in the direction leading away from the crime scene. They agreed to turn around after twenty minutes and meet back at Scott's car.

The cool morning air and dawn light were a welcome change of mood for Molly. The drops of dew were so pretty on the leaves and grass in the early hours of light. She admired the artistry of spiders but tried not to actually look for the arachnids. Molly sipped her travel mug of coffee with a touch of cream plus a few melted chocolate chips. Coffee with chocolate was her favorite daily combination. Molly checked her phone again for the twenty-minute timer. She only had a few minutes before she should turn around and wondered if she should text Scott to keep going because she was enjoying the quiet of nature so much.

Her headlamp lit up something shiny in the leaves along the side of the trail. It took Molly aback when she saw it. Litter was very rare on this stretch of trail. A dedicated hiking club affiliated with the Buckeye Trail Association meticulously maintained the trail, and Molly often felt guilty for not joining and attending the local chapter meetings. Without thinking, she bent down to inspect the shiny object. Molly wasn't a germaphobe, but picking up litter with her bare hands also wasn't something she usually did. Awkwardly using the bottom of her mug to shift the damp leaves, she uncovered an earring. No longer worried about germs, Molly picked it up and adjusted her headlamp to see it clearly.

She knew this earring. It was a rose-gold hoop very similar to the earrings that Shannon had worn the day before, with two strands of metal filament twisted together. Goosebumps sprouted on Molly's arms, despite her jacket. She looked around, suddenly feeling like someone was watching her from among the trees. This early there should be other trail users, but she had only seen one other person since starting out. Her phone alarm went off. Molly jumped, almost dropping both her coffee and the earring.

Pocketing the rose-gold hoop, Molly turned around to walk back to the trailhead. Was it really Shannon's earring? What time had Shannon been in the shop the day before? Molly couldn't place when her cousin was there—was it before or after the drama with the trail runner and the police? It must have been before. Was she wearing both earrings when she was there, or just one? Molly did distinctly remember her wearing a hoop just like this and also remembered noticing the sweat on her neck. Was Shannon on the trail yesterday when Trevor was, too? But it was the wrong direction, the wrong side of the trail. The damaged bridge was on the other side of the trailhead, Trevor's belongings had been found nearby on that side. Shannon was not an outdoor enthusiast and was unlikely to spend any time on the local trails. In fact, Molly was sure that Shannon didn't even own hiking boots. A few minutes later, she heard Scott's familiar heavy running gait behind her and swung her head around to look over her shoulder. She must have really slowed her own walking speed if he was already catching up to her.

"Hey there, pokey," Scott said, adjusting his pace to walk next to her, and patted her back. She still had goosebumps. He was breathing hard but gave her a quick kiss on the temple, which he knew she did not want to return because he smelled and was sweaty. She smiled at his guarded affection for her benefit.

"Scott, I can't believe this. I think I just found

Shannon's earring on the trail," she told him and took it out of her pocket.

"Well, that seems unlikely. Shannon?"

"She was wearing earrings exactly like this yesterday. I know she was."

"Seems crazy that she'd be on the trail the same day of a big incident," Scott said as he took the earring and held it up in the light of his headlamp. The sky was brightening, and the trail was nearly fully visible.

"Do you think she's okay? Maybe she's missing like Trevor and we don't even know? Maybe the same person kidnapped them both. Do you think I should tell the police?" Molly asked, biting her lip. The worry that had been rolling around in her mind forced her to continue. "Or do you think Shannon has something to do with Trevor being missing? Like, she's somehow involved with his disappearance?" She didn't know what she was thinking. She felt like everyone was a suspect and hated how responsible she felt for whatever had happened to Trevor.

"I mean, I don't think you need to jump to the very worst conclusion, even though she is Shannon. Call her or text to see if she responds. And if she doesn't, maybe you should tell Joe. He's a detective and might even get assigned to the case. Maybe you can tell him in an unofficial capacity? You don't have to blame Shannon. Just inform Joe about your concern." Joe was May's husband and served on their local police force. Scott handed the earring back to Molly.

"That's a good idea. I'll call her in another couple of hours. She never seems to be awake very early."

"Yeah. We don't need two people missing on the Buckeye Trail. Tell me what you find out later today. I'm going to finish up." Scott patted her shoulder again and continued running.

Molly bit her lip again. Could two people really have gone missing on the trail? Could Shannon have kidnapped Trevor?

Molly arrived back at the parking lot outside the garden center well after Scott. It seemed that he had already finished with his post-run stretching routine because he was looking at his phone. Molly had thought of nothing beyond the earring during the rest of her walk and flipped it mindlessly between her fingers. She had made the decision that she needed to tell her twin sister about the find. Her mind always worked best in tandem with May's.

"I forgot I need to pick up a book at the library today," Scott mumbled to Molly as they stowed their headlamps in the trunk of his car. "I got an email reminder. Too bad they're not open now." Molly wasn't really paying attention, her mind more on the earring than books. Scott was an avid reader and very much preferred the feel of a real paper book to an e-reader. In fact, he collected fancy hardbacks with gilded spines. Molly thought a Kindle was just fine for reading herself but enjoyed the hunt for the golden books as gifts for her bookish husband.

"What do you think?" Scott said as he slammed the trunk closed, jolting Molly out of her worries about Shannon. "Should I make bacon and pancakes for breakfast? Or should we stop by the café for an even greasier first meal?" He was smiling broadly, proud of this unhealthy decision so early in the morning after a run.

"I like the idea of your pancakes and bacon this morning, Scotty." She kissed his sweaty mouth despite herself.

6

SUCCULENT PLANTING AND A RING BOX

After a long, warm shower and with a belly full of carbs and fat, Molly arrived at the garden center earlier than her normal starting time. Usually, she was the first one at the center at 8:00 a.m. Theo had early morning soccer practice nearly every day, and May was getting her kids ready for school. Molly enjoyed the solitude and quiet of the place before they opened at nine. The strong floral and soil scents always struck her as she entered the shop. Every time, the smell centered her and reminded her of their late grandparents. She involuntarily inhaled deeply as she entered the store in the morning.

Sherlock emerged from the back of the shop, bleary-eyed, and stretched his black-and-white kitty body as far as it would go. He sauntered over to Molly and wrapped his tail around her legs. "Good morning, Mr. Sherlock," she said, petting him from ears to tail in one sweep. This was also part of her morning routine: being greeted by Sherlock and filling his water and food bowls behind the counter. She knew that he also nagged whoever opened the shop on Saturday to feed him, and that person doled out an extra scoop in the bowl for Sunday.

After inhaling half of his bowl of kitty kibble, Sherlock ambled into the shoppable greenhouse section of the store. He found a sunny spot to nap between some of the shade-loving annuals and perennials. Since they'd been restocked in the spring, Sherlock seemed to consider pink impatiens his nap buddies. Molly didn't understand why the kitty left the houseplants in the greenhouse alone but was grateful that he didn't chomp on them. As children, she and May had cats that were always taking nibbles of their mother's spider plants and *Monstera*.

Molly wandered into the staff-only greenhouse, located in the back of the building and off-limits to customers. The back area of the store also contained a cramped staff break room, the employee restroom, and a storage room. She separated a few tomato plants into individual pots. The succulent cuttings under grow lights on one shelf were doing especially well. She needed to separate out the succulents that she would sell at the Saturday morning Farmer's Market, but before she did, Molly said in a soft but confident voice, "You are the most beautiful succulents. You are such good growers, and I love you all." Grandma Patty used to say positive affirmations to growing plants, and she had wonderful success. Molly carried on the tradition, especially because they were always in such high demand. She worked her way down, addressing each shelf. It seemed she was always growing succulents. The number of cacti and aloe vera they sold at the shop and at the market still surprised her. Didn't people in Hawthorn Heights already have enough of the little plants?

Molly was crouched down, addressing the bottom shelf of baby succulents, when she heard the front door chime. They were not open yet, and she didn't know who to expect. She couldn't remember if she had locked the door behind her, as she usually did in the mornings.

"Good morning," Theo called before Molly heard the door swing closed behind him. He shed his jacket before he entered the back room, swinging it onto their employee coat hooks on the wooden paneling of the workroom with muscle memory, not looking.

"Hey there. You're here early," Molly said to Theo as she moved over to the worktable with a tray of the most mature succulents. She felt silly talking to the plants in front of him and abandoned her affirmations. At least there was only one shelf left without positive thoughts.

"I forgot to tell you," Theo said, leaning against the stainless steel worktable, arms crossed. "Coach canceled practice this morning. I figured I'd come in early. I didn't sleep so well last night after everything. How are you holding up?"

"I tossed and turned a lot and had weird dreams," Molly replied. Theo looked as sleep-deprived as she was, with slightly red eyes surrounded by puffy skin.

"Yeah, yeah. Me, too. Do you have any more news about Trevor? Nothing in the local news. I really thought there'd be something."

"I don't have any new info. I was thinking of calling Joe later today, though."

"Seems like a good idea," Theo said.

"He might know something, at least. And didn't one of the police officers say something about a detective following up with us? That whole couple of hours is a bit of a blur to me still."

"I hear you. Such a weird afternoon." Theo let out a long breath. "Yeah, I think they said something about a detective calling if they wanted more information. I don't think we have anything more to provide, though." Theo pushed away from the worktable. "So, uh, before I work on some restocking, I thought I should show you what I picked up after work last night, even after all the chaos." Theo's demeanor turned from concerned to nervous, an unusual state for him.

"Oh, really?" Molly's eyebrows raised expectantly,

her hands frozen in place in their succulent sorting.

"Yeah. I don't feel like I have a good enough plan yet, but I figure I should keep it with me in case the ideal situation arises." Theo pulled a small box out of his pocket. Then he turned the box over and gave it a little shake. He extracted a velvet box out of it as one would separate Russian nesting dolls. The distinctive popping sound of the ring box opening gave Molly a shiver of excitement. Engagement rings held such hope for the future.

"Theo, it's beautiful!"

"She has a thing for white gold. I found a place in Cleveland that uses recycled gold, so that's cool. And I figured I should get as many diamonds as I could afford, but she deserves more." Theo's attention was on the floor, not on the ring.

"Vivian will love it. It's perfect!" Molly realized she was smiling wider than she had in the past twenty-four hours. Theo smiled back, although he still lacked his usual confidence. Molly admired Theo's girlfriend immensely. Vivian was working on her PhD while also treating patients with psychiatric issues. Molly thought her dark skin was beautiful and was jealous of her long braids that held charms and beads.

"I think she'll like it. I talked to her aunt about what she wanted and stuff. Anyway, I wanted to show you."

"And you'll tell me when that ideal situation arises?" Molly asked.

"You know I will," Theo said as he tucked the boxes back together. "I'll work on the mulch restock now. Let me know if you need anything."

Molly heard him move around the front of the store and continued with her work, humming, now with much more on her mind than just succulents.

Molly was practiced at planting succulents en masse. First, she filled a variety of small, decorative pots halfway with her standard succulent mixture of sand and soil. She went back down the assembly line and poked a divot in each container of soil, one by one. Then she plopped a little grey-green plant in each pot, working down the row. Finally, she surrounded the individual plants with more of the soil-sand mixture, gently patting down the soil around the roots with her fingertips and below each fleshy leaf. This solitary, silent work felt joyful and productive, her mind on her work and not on the missing college student and her cousin.

Molly also had to put together the living flower arrangement by this afternoon. Archie had followed up with some texts, and they had agreed to meet at the Home and Garden Show at 10:00 a.m. That meant Molly needed to get her "something purple with three succulents" arrangement done before then.

Molly cleared off her stainless steel workspace, doing a second pass with a soft cloth to remove all the gritty sand and soil. She chose a wide ceramic pot glazed in bright royal purple for her foundation. She would place many pots of plants inside this large one, and customers could divide them up after their event was over. Instead of using bulky chunks of floral foam to secure the pots in place, which could not be recycled and were made of plastic, Molly usually opted for a mix of moss and shredded newspaper, which could be composted or recycled when it was time to divide up the arrangement. Sometimes she used chicken wire to hold the pots in place, or just a grid of floral tape if her plants crowded themselves into place well enough. Above the individual pots, she placed dried moss or curly Spanish moss.

Molly selected some already potted succulents, a stack of twigs, and a few small pots of annual garden plants—light purple violas and yellow kalanchoe. The kalanchoe was a bit like a succulent and would pair well with them. She also chose bright-green indoor pothos for added texture and greenery. She soaked the twigs in water so they would bend easily. The different shades of purple with a few pops of yellow came together well with a light purple *Graptopetalum* succulent and an *Echeveria tolimanensis* that was light green with purple tones. She couldn't decide what the third succulent should be: probably a more standard green. The color combinations delighted Molly, and she found herself humming while she worked.

7

WHISPERED CONVERSATIONS AND DARK CHOCOLATE MOCHA

The morning passed in a tired blur with new and known customers. One of their regulars, Claire, visited with her bachelor neighbor to buy annuals for their side-by-side patios in the town's condo complex. Molly was happy to advise and chat with the pair. Between customers, Molly and May held whispered conversations about the earring Molly found and how to respond.

"I didn't get a great look at Shannon, as usual," May told Molly as she inspected the earring. "I try not to make eye contact, you know. I just remember her scarf and thought it was so weird and unseasonably warm. In June, I wouldn't wear something around my neck. And the whole thing about patting Hannah's head was so rude. Hannah said so when we got in the car. I always try to make Shannon out to be less of a bad guy than I think she is to the kids. It's not easy."

"So you don't know if she was wearing two earrings yesterday or just one?" Molly asked, trying to steer the conversation away from May's constant negativity about their cousin. Sherlock wrapped his body and tail around Molly's legs while she chatted with her sister. She absently ran her fingers along his fur.

"I don't know. But what would she ever be doing on the trail? She's just not a hiker, not into being outside or in nature."

"Right. She'd never be hiking in those heels," Molly replied. They giggled. Molly was always giggling with May, even in serious conversations. They both looked around, trying not to disturb customers in their garden planning and wanderings.

"She could have different shoes in her Lexus. It's got an enormous trunk, I'm sure," May offered in a lower whisper.

"I suppose so. I texted her right before the shop opened, and she hasn't replied. I'm getting worried. Do you think I should tell the police? I don't know it's hers for sure or when it got lost on the trail. It wasn't even near the broken bridge."

"I do like your idea of asking Joe. He's not assigned to the case right now, so he's not directly involved. I think you can just ask his opinion and see what he says," May told Molly. "You'd think I would have picked up on some of this detective stuff after being married to him for eight years, but I sure haven't. He'll have some advice to share, at least."

"Okay. I'll call him on the way to the Home and Garden Show."

A few minutes later, Molly found herself helping another regular customer, Mr. Davidson. He had retired a few years ago from a factory job and now worked odd jobs around Hawthorn Heights and the surrounding communities as a handyman. He stopped by frequently, sometimes three times a week, to buy bird seed. Mr. Davidson was a strong older man who always declined Theo's help. Today, he was in quite a mood.

"I'm a' thinkin' of changin' things up at my bird feedin' station," he told Molly. "Been gettin' too many mangy squirrels hangin' on the feeder. It's almos' broken."

"Well, do you want to get a feeder that is more secure, or do you want to welcome the squirrels and feed them some corn of their own?" Molly admired his dark hair. She thought he had less gray than she did, even though he was probably more than thirty years her senior.

"No, I don't want those varmints in my yard at all! If I had my way, I'd a' get rid of 'em altogether. Let 'em stay out in the woods, not our neighborhoods. We sure got a lot of 'em out in these forests 'round town. I need a new feeder or a dif'rnt mountin' pole. What do you have here?"

Molly showed him the baffles they sold that he could put on his pole so the squirrels couldn't climb it, as well as some bird feeders that only allowed lightweight visitors to eat the food, excluding both squirrels and chipmunks. He stayed for some time, considering, and ended up buying both products.

After Mr. Davidson shuffled out the door with his purchases, Molly, May, and Theo observed a group of police officers talking in the parking lot the garden center shared with the trailhead, along with what looked like civilians. May identified those without uniforms as detectives, like Joe, who wore civilian clothing on the job. Molly thought that having extra minds working the case to find Trevor was a good thing. After a few minutes, the group walked up the trail toward the broken bridge.

Soon after the police arrived, so did Glenn, the owner of the hiking store next door, the Trail Guide. Despite the ample trail time he put in, Glenn was a heavyset man. He towered over Molly. She often wondered how many customers his shop brought in because he visited Patty's Plant Place nearly every day to chat with whoever was working.

"You guys left early yesterday, huh?" Glenn said, as a greeting to May.

"I wasn't here, but Molly and Theo could fill you in about the hiker that went missing." May's eyes darted to Theo to ask him to explain the situation. Picking up on May's plea, he recounted the events of the evening before.

"I saw the cop cars, but we had a ton of stock to put out and lots of customers too," Glenn said to the three of them. Molly remembered seeing the semi pull into their parking lot next door the afternoon before. "Wasn't a good time to stop over. I don't like that a hiker was in distress on our trail. Bad for tourism. This is a safe trail, a safe town. I came over later to hear about it, but the shop was closed up."

"I know it's bad for business to close without warning, but none of us wanted to make Charlotte and Ryan stay," Molly put in. "It was kind of a mental health call."

"I'm not chiding you for closing. Just wanted to stop over and hear the story. That trail makes my business, and I want to make sure it's seen in a good light."

"Yeah, yeah. We hear you, man," Theo agreed. "It's important to all of us."

Molly needed to leave for the Home and Garden Show but felt unsure about leaving the comfort of the shop to spend a few hours in a vast crowd of people with someone she only emailed regularly and had only met in person once. She said goodbye to Glenn and left the shop in the competent hands of May and Theo. Theo practically pushed her out the door.

The Broken Bridge

Before leaving town, Molly stopped by the Scottish Ferret to get another jolt of caffeine in the form of a dark chocolate mocha. Then she called Joe as she drove and sipped her coffee.

"Hey, Joe, I know you're at work. I just have a detective question that needs answering," Molly told her brother-in-law when he answered. She had known Joe for more than a decade and often sought his advice on general life problems. His grandparents on both sides had immigrated to the United States from Japan, and so he spoke a little Japanese and knew some ancestral recipes. Joe's Japanese dishes were among Scott's favorites. Both Hannah and Noah had inherited Joe's thick, extra-straight, beautifully inky black hair.

"Well, if it's a detective question, you might as well ask me while I'm at the precinct. Does this have to do with the incident on the trail yesterday?" Joe guessed.

"You got me. It does."

"I'm not assigned to the case, and I'm not at liberty to tell you anything that the department hasn't released to the press yet," Joe told her in a practiced, official tone that was rather unfamiliar.

"Oh, I'm not trying to get more info out of you. I just found something, and I'm not sure if I should tell the detective who has been assigned to the case. I don't actually know who that is yet. The police officers we talked to yesterday said a detective might contact us today, but no one has yet." Molly felt a bit on edge, almost nervous, and realized she'd used more words than she normally would. It was silly to be nervous with Joe, she told herself.

"Okay. I'm happy to advise," Joe replied, his voice friendly but still professional.

Molly turned on her blinker and steered the van onto the on ramp to the highway. "I found an earring on the trail this morning. Scott and I were there early, before the sun came all the way up. It glinted in my headlamp. The thing is, Shannon was wearing an earring that looked just like it yesterday—after Trevor came in. Trevor is the boy who is missing, assuming he hasn't been found yet, of course. I hope he has. Anyway, I haven't heard from Shannon. I'm worried that she might be missing too since it might be her earring that I found on the trail." Molly still felt like she was blabbering.

Joe made a thoughtful noise. "That is interesting. Was it anywhere near the broken bridge?" he asked.

"No, it wasn't near the bridge at all. We went the other way."

"So because it was not in the vicinity of the incident, you're not sure if it's evidence or not. I can see why you wouldn't be sure what to do," Joe said.

"And also not sure who to tell. I probably should stop by Shannon's house or her work to make sure she's okay. She hasn't responded to my texts. I don't want to get Shannon in trouble if she's not missing.

I'm not really sure the earring is hers. But I know she was wearing earrings just like it yesterday."

"Things are always more complicated with Shannon, aren't they?" Joe chuckled. "First, we have not found Trevor. Sorry I can't set your mind at ease there. Like I said, Moll, I'm not on the case, but I heard some basics in our morning meeting. We can't call her a missing person until someone has filed a report or placed a call like the runner did for Trevor. I don't think it would hurt to collect the earring as evidence, which could help if we find out she is missing. But if she's not, by no means do we need to tell her you found the earring if it ends up implicating her. It could have been anyone if you found it in a public location. And she was out in public yesterday wearing them, so any number of people could have seen her with the earrings."

"Okay. I'll try to call her again in a few hours. I hope she's okay." Molly thought for a moment. "So you think I should drop off the earring at the precinct? I could this afternoon, but hopefully I'll hear from Shannon before that. And do you think I should file a missing person's report?"

"I think you need to confirm that Shannon is missing first. And I think you might as well turn in the earring. Also, she may have been on the trail and may know something more that we don't."

"Oh, that's true." Molly brightened. "She could be a witness. She could have seen something, but didn't really know what it was at the time. Shannon could know something about what happened to Trevor." After a beat, she added in a lower tone: "Joe, she really couldn't have hurt Trevor. She couldn't push a hiker over a bridge."

"We don't know what happened there yesterday. We don't know if he did get pushed over the bridge. We don't even know where Trevor is yet. He's a missing person right now."

8

THE HOME AND GARDEN SHOW AND LUNCH

Molly got a bit of a "too friendly" vibe from Archie as soon as he met her at the entrance to the convention center with her ticket. Too big of a smile and way too much eye contact. Scott would have been on diligent-husband guard in this situation. Archie wasn't flirting, exactly, just weirdly *so* happy. Molly had talked on the phone with the man only a few times, but they had exchanged emails frequently for her monthly column. Was he always like this, and she just hadn't seen it because they weren't face-to-face?

Archie escorted her to the check-in table, where a registration worker gave Molly a tote bag containing numerous flyers and random magnets and pens that she didn't want. She almost tried to give it back but assumed it would be rude. At least the bag contained a map of the exhibits—which she certainly needed

—along with a wristband for entry. This check-in station felt expansive and bright to Molly. There were so many people, and there was so much to see.

"So, I've spent the morning in the Erie Room, and I think we should both check out the Huron Room together, which is just down the steps over there," Archie said, barely taking a breath, while he stood much too close. "The vendors in the Huron Room are more directed to product sellers such as yourself, so I'd really like your expertise there." He pointed at her flowery map of the convention center to show her where they would go. She could smell coffee on his breath.

"Makes sense to me," Molly responded flatly. She was trying to convey a very strong "no flirt" vibe. "So, are you looking for new products for advertisers or to highlight in a story?" She had to stand close to him in order to hear his response, unfortunately.

"Both. I'm looking for new products and companies to partner with to show off their brands, products, and so forth in the magazine," he said with a huge smile. "I do like to see their wares in person and start a personal relationship with the company staff instead of just looking at pictures online. Like meeting you here instead of just having a relationship online and via email."

"I do agree that it's easier to judge a product you can touch than only what you can see in a picture," she said, hoping he understood she was talking about gardening and definitely not about relating to colleagues.

And so Molly spent an hour and a half perusing the booths with Archie following her around. He didn't so much as go with her as let her lead him from booth to booth.

Molly felt like everyone was too close to her, not only Archie. Such large—but enclosed—spaces with vast throngs of people she didn't know made Molly feel claustrophobic and uneasy. High ceilings and bright lights made it worse. The many smells, chatter, and bright colors clashed—together they provided too much sensory input.

But the flowers.

She was surrounded by what she loved.

Molly was dizzy with new information. She visited booths of new brands of environmentally friendly fertilizer and pesticides that she considered stocking in the shop. A man with an extravagant mustache spent an entire ten minutes telling her and Archie about his never-before-released, extra-strong deer-repelling marigolds bred specifically for this purpose. His sales pitch sold her on that product, too. Although Molly ached to have time one-on-one with these vendors, instead of twenty-to-one, she loved every topic, every vendor, every product. She'd be picky about what they'd actually sell at the store, but she saw the same value that Archie did in visiting the Home and Garden show.

In the future, she might make a habit of attending the annual show during the least busy time of the event. May or Theo might even enjoy attending with her. Molly loved people watching, and this place certainly had such a variety of garden enthusiasts. Molly especially admired a child's stroller decked out with silk flowers for the event.

By the time Archie announced they should head out for lunch, Molly felt like she had spent an entire day there, but one look at her watch told her it had only been the hour and a half they had decided on. Somehow, she felt both exhausted and energized by the new contacts, products, ideas, and inspiration she'd found there. She was glad that she had a notebook to help her remember all of it. The back pocket of her jeans was full of business cards. But her phone had no new texts or calls to indicate Shannon's whereabouts.

Archie led the way out of the convention center and into a small, upscale restaurant a few blocks away. It struck Molly that he seemed to know his way around the metro center better than she did. The short walk offered sunshine and warm air that cleansed Molly after such a busy, people-filled morning.

Greensward was apparently named after Frederick Law Olmsted's first design for Central Park, although it was in the heart of Cleveland, nowhere near New York City. The space felt absolutely upscale compared to her old standby, the Scottish Ferret. The tables at Greensward were laid with thick fabric tablecloths topped with glass goblets turned on their heads, silverware folded into starkly white cloth napkins, and votives in metal candle holders. Greensward's walls featured large, framed, splash art that depicted trees and leaves in matching yellow-and-green color palettes. Within seconds of entering the chilly, air-conditioned establishment, Molly wished she had her zip-up hoodie from the van.

After they were seated, Archie sat studying the menu, which was in a paper folder that Molly expected was reprinted frequently because of how clean it was. He fidgeted with the metal corners while reading. She selected a salmon wedge salad, which was much more expensive than her normal budget for eating out, but it was somewhat close to her beloved fish tacos. Molly took a deep breath and rubbed her cold arms. It was good to sit after so much jostling, even if she was chilly. Archie finally settled on their lunch special of the day, which sounded like a gussied-up sandwich with multiple cold cuts and brined vegetables. The extremely slim waitress practically popped out of the hardwood floor to take their order when Archie closed his menu folder. She returned quickly with warm bread.

"What an event, huh!" Archie said. It wasn't a question, and it was the shortest thing he had said yet that day.

"It was an enormous show, that's for sure," Molly agreed. "You could spend days and days visiting vendors." Molly was glad for the warmth of the carbs and butter.

"Some people do spend days and days at home and gardens shows. I wish I had more time, but we can't visit the entirety of every show, unfortunately. They are held in nearly every state in America, sometimes more than once a year. *Gardening Tomorrow* will rent a booth at a few of them near our headquarters, but most are scouting ventures for us. I'm really glad to get your input for the magazine. Tell me which vendors you liked the most." Archie spoke so quickly that Molly felt like she was still catching up several seconds after he stopped talking. She blinked at him, unsure how to respond.

At a loss for words, Molly opened her notebook and paged through her scribbles from the morning. Archie watched expectantly, even leaning forward and trying to read her notes upside down. "I did really like those marigolds," she said finally. Her brief response felt feeble, and she stared at her notes, trying to find something else to report.

"They were quite innovative! What a great, natural way to deter nuisance fauna without harming them—or the plants or soil. They really would make a great feature story that you could write and I expect the vendor would be happy to connect with…"

Soil.

Molly suddenly remembered during Archie's verbose wanderings that she wanted to know whether he had actually visited the trail or not when Trevor was on it. His hiking boots had looked both muddy and also brand new. But he hadn't actually said if he'd been hiking or not, just that he wanted to go. She realized he was still talking, and so she nodded and pasted on a thoughtful face. Archie didn't seem to notice that she wasn't being attentive. When he took a breath, she said the first thing she could think of to steer the conversation in the direction she wanted.

"So, what do you think of Ohio? Have you been here before?"

"I have been to Cleveland before, but not your small town of Hawthorn Heights. Ohio is a really beautiful state with such a variety of habitats. It's so interesting that there's a different USDA Plant Hardiness Zone right in the middle of the state—that's quite unusual. I have been to Columbus as well, the state capital, for another home and garden show a few years ago." My goodness, this man could talk. She decided to just cut to the chase and interrupted him.

"Didn't you mention something about wanting to hike the Buckeye Trail?" Molly asked. Then she thought it sounded too direct and added, "Do you hike often?"

"Oh, it's something I always tell myself I need to do. I want to be a hiker. I saw that the Buckeye Trail cut right through Hawthorn Heights and thought I should try to hike it while I was in town to visit. It's a well-known trail and obviously specific to Ohio, something special. I expect you do a lot of hiking with the trail right beside your shop, and I'd really love it if you could show me your favorite part of the trail while I'm here."

She quickly decided to just ignore the invitation and talk about what she knew. "The Buckeye Trail is beautiful and makes a big circle through the entire state. It's quite beloved. There are towns that hold annual celebrations or races. It's very well maintained and marked." There was an unexpected pause. She wasn't sure if he thought she would say something else, or if he didn't actually have a response. Was he mad she didn't jump at the chance to hike with him? She was composing a question about being on the trail when Trevor went missing in her head, but Archie spoke before she did.

"Such a shame about that young man. Have you heard any updates?" he asked, as if reading her mind.

"I know nothing more than I did last night, really. It doesn't feel like it was just yesterday afternoon." She wasn't getting the information she wanted. Maybe she was being too nosy. Perhaps she should let the detectives decide who was a suspect and who wasn't.

"I agree that the time I spent at your garden shop seems a lot farther away than just yesterday. I've never been part of a police investigation and wasn't sure if I should have stayed or not. It was a very odd way to meet you, to be sure," Archie said. The food arrived, and the pair dropped the conversation about Trevor and hiking. Molly felt like the food had taken forever, and her mouth was watering when the waitress put the plate in front of her.

Molly's salad had the smallest wedge she had ever seen—there was no way it was actually a quarter of a head of iceberg lettuce. However, it was extremely satisfying to cut right through even this small portion. The perfectly seasoned salmon and the house-made blue cheese dressing were a delicious paring. She was halfway done eating it when she realized she hadn't said a single thing since the waitress had laid down their plates. Archie just kept continuing to talk about the Home and Garden Show without expecting or needing any response from her, apparently. Her mind kept wandering to the two errands she needed to do before actually returning to work: her earring drop off at the police station and then the flower delivery. She checked her watch. Somehow, they had been at the restaurant for an entire hour. She attempted to pay more attention to Archie and made some more agreeable noises between bites.

In the end, Molly ate her meal much quicker

than Archie, who just kept talking and nibbling at his sandwich and French fries. She finished eating and checked her watch again. She really needed to get going. Archie managed to notice.

"You really plowed through that salad. It must have been good. My own meal is really terrific, if I do say so." he told her. She knew he had something else to say and interrupted him before he could go on.

"I should get back to the shop. I have a few deliveries I have to make this afternoon."

"I can cover the check, if you want to just get going. No problem there. I'm spending the rest of the afternoon at the Home and Garden Show, and they'll all still be there for a while," he said with a smile.

"You don't have to pay for my lunch. I'll call over the waitress." Molly looked around the restaurant and only saw other lunchers. The twiggy waitress who had been so attentive early in their meal was now nowhere to be found.

"You can pay for me next time. I'm around all weekend," he said succinctly, and actually winked. Molly finally agreed to let him pay just so she could leave sooner. She had no intention of sharing another meal with this chatty man this weekend or any time in the future.

9

A VOICEMAIL AND A STATELY DELIVERY

It was a relief to be in the flower delivery van by herself. Molly didn't even turn on music or a podcast on the way to the police station. She needed the quiet after the busyness of the morning and the buzzing of the weird lunch.

While she drove, Molly considered why she felt so safe at the garden center. It was actually the only place she'd ever worked, other than the campus coffee shop in college. Molly had worked a few hours a week with Grandma Patty and Grandpa Will at the garden center during high school, while May had gotten a job at their local library shelving books. Grandma Patty shared her interest in flowers and gardening with both twins and Shannon at an early age, but Molly's passion grew stronger than the other girls'. Molly attended the Ohio State University Agricultural Technical Institute and majored in horticulture. May went to the nearby Ohio State University campus and majored in accounting and then got a job at a local tax service firm two towns over from Hawthorn Heights. Molly couldn't understand May's love of numbers.

After college, Molly never even considered working anywhere besides the garden center and just started right back where she left off with Grandma at Patty's Plant Place. Grandpa had died while the twins were in college, which was hard on all of them. It felt wonderful to help Grandma with the shop in his absence. Molly was the one who started selling the living flower arrangements, and Grandma loved them. When Grandma died six years ago, May came to work at the shop too and was glad for fewer hours so she could stay home with her kids more. And so the garden center was like a second home. Molly missed her grandma, but she still saw her fingerprints and influence throughout the shop, especially the name, of course.

A half hour later, Molly was in the police station parking lot. She flipped the rose-gold hoop earring around in her fingers again. Was it Shannon's? Should she turn it in? Would it get Shannon in trouble? Where was Shannon? Molly sat a while in indecision in the van's air-conditioning and finally hit Shannon's number on her phone screen to call her. No answer. She waited for the voicemail greeting to play. She almost hung up.

"Uh, hey, Shannon. It's Molly. Just wanted to check in about the stuff that happened yesterday on the trail. You probably heard about the hiker that went missing. He was in the shop a bit before the bridge was reported, um, broken. We were all questioned by the police. Me and Theo and Charlotte, anyway. Just wanted to make sure you knew." And she clicked off. That wasn't what she meant to say at all.

She flipped the earring around some more. It really looked like the pair she knew Shannon was wearing the day before. Molly decided to go the route of less confrontation but still see if she could find an answer about it. She took a picture of the earring in her hand and made sure that the van's interior was cropped out of the view. She didn't know why she didn't want Shannon to know she was in the van, but she definitely didn't want Shannon to know she was in the parking lot of the police station.

"Forgot to say in my message: found this earring and thought it might be yours?" She texted Shannon with the picture. That would do it. No mention of the trail. No mention of Trevor. No accusation. It kind of sounded like she may have found it in the shop. And she didn't actually have to talk to Shannon. This was better. Shannon would probably respond if she was missing the earring and not ignore her as she had so far. If she wasn't missing herself, that was.

Molly decided that she'd deliver the earring after

the flowers. That would give Shannon some time to reply, and if she hadn't in a few hours, then Molly would turn it in to the police. She plopped the earring in the cup holder of the van and threw the gear into reverse.

With her foot still on the brake and her hand still on the gearshift, she paused. Oh. Except now Shannon would know that it was Molly who gave the earring to the police. No more anonymity, like Joe had said. Molly put the van back in park and put her hand to her forehead and leaned on it. She really should have thought about this longer. Why was her relationship with her cousin so complicated? Now she'd just have to wait for Shannon to reply. If it was hers, she'd return the earring, but if Shannon didn't claim it, then Molly would give it to the police. She wouldn't know if Shannon was lying or not, but at least she had tried. It was better this way.

Back at the shop, May was extremely interested in all the new products and vendors Molly could report about, but knew that she needed to collect the living arrangement and head out to deliver it on time. They only talked briefly before Molly hopped back in the van, the plants well tethered in the back.

Still no response from Shannon as Molly and the grouping of flowers and succulents traveled to a neighboring town, Oakville Heights.

When making flower or plant deliveries, Patty's Plant Place staff always wore a branded yellow-and-

The Broken Bridge

blue hat to look more official. The staff members had magnetic nametags that they wore in the shop, but they weren't strict about wearing them all the time. Grandma Patty and Grandpa Will always asked employees wear navy blue aprons but Molly found hers so uncomfortable that she did away with them after Grandma Patty passed. For deliveries, Molly just kept a few hats in the van, and it worked. As it was, Molly made most of the deliveries.

Molly found the address easily enough, but she couldn't see the house from the road, only a winding driveway with a gate. It must be a pain to pull the recycling and trash bins to the curb, Molly thought. They'd probably have to use a golf cart or something.

She donned her hat, and continued up the driveway in the van. As Molly rounded the last curve in the drive, her mouth fell open, and she slowed to a stop.

The home was immense, with arches everywhere. There were tall gray stone arches supporting the roof of the front porch, or whatever word you'd use to describe the entrance to such a stately house. The gray arches repeated above doorway-size windows on both sides of the house, eight of them on each side. There was no telling how many rooms the windows represented. Arch after arch of wisteria ran along a garden winding from the south side of the home as well, and the house itself arched out of a hillside. It didn't have a steep roof but an arched roof, rounded at the top.

She hoped that her succulent and flower arrangement would be fancy enough for people who lived in such a richly designed and ornate house. Violas and pathos, even when paired with trendy succulents, might seem too simple in such a formal setting. She finished her crawl up the rest of the driveway and parked right in front of the ever-so-fancy front "porch." Would a butler answer the door?

Molly could see the doorbell camera and did her best not to look directly at it as she waited for someone to answer. A cheery woman greeted her in less than a minute.

"Oh, this is so lovely!" she exclaimed without greeting Molly. The woman was a few years older than Molly and exquisitely dressed in shades of navy and bright pink. At least she seemed to enjoy some color, Molly thought. "Your shop is just the sweetest place, and I knew you would come up with something smart and perky for our table tonight." She smiled at Molly. "We're having out-of-town guests," she added after a beat.

"I'm thrilled you like it. The order said purple with some succulents, and that's what I did." Flowers and plants had a way of helping her connect to people she wouldn't usually feel comfortable talking to. "I guess I literally delivered what you had in mind." Molly enjoyed her own joke with a chuckle as she gingerly handed over the pot of plants.

"How wonderful that the person who put the flowers together also personally delivered them. Thank you so much." Then her smile faded, and she continued, "But my goodness. I just heard on the radio, on our local National Public Radio station, that your shop was the center of a lot of activity last night. I guess the story was on about an hour ago. How dreadful."

Molly's breath caught in her throat. "Oh. Yes."

"There was an accident on the trail, the reporter said. A missing boy?"

"Yes, he's missing," Molly told her, her heart racing. "A young man, really. He was—is—going to be a senior in college this year." She didn't know why her body was reacting in such a way. This woman was kind and was just curious.

"I hope they find him. Do you know if there are any leads?"

"They're not telling us much at all. We were all interviewed, but there wasn't a lot to say. I don't know anything myself." For some reason, Molly purposely left out the fact that she'd met the young man and hung out with him, even when she offered that she knew Trevor's age.

Satisfied with her answer, the woman smiled and told her, "Well, I'll be following the story as much as my schedule will allow. I hope they find him soon."

Molly looked down at the flowers and admired them again. She felt another rush of happiness and mentally let them go. "There's a card in there. We always include some care information for the plants."

"How thoughtful. Thank you again," the customer said, her tone final but kind.

Molly stopped at Shannon's house on the way to the shop but saw nothing of interest. Shannon usually parked in the garage, and Molly had no way of knowing if her SUV was parked inside or not. Shannon's real estate agency was a twenty-minute drive in the other direction. Molly considered making a detour, but returned to her own place of work instead.

Molly drove with the radio dialed to the local NPR station, half hoping to hear a repeat of the story that her customer had heard but not really listening. So the news was out. Trevor was officially missing. And Shannon had neither surfaced nor claimed the earring.

10

TESTS AND TOMATOES

Saturday morning was one Molly had highlighted on her calendar for two weeks. It was the morning she needed to take a pregnancy test, to see if this month they had finally conceived or not. It was both exciting and nerve-racking, but this ritual had also become commonplace since she had done it month after month for almost a year. She and Scott had been trying for long enough that she was expecting to be let down again. It was easier not to really anticipate the two pink lines on the pregnancy test indicating a growing baby, when only one pink line showed up each and every cycle, meaning that her period would start any day.

Her bladder woke her, and she rolled out of bed before Scott was awake, tiptoeing into the bathroom. Knowing that half the battle was holding it until she could pee on the pregnancy test, Molly had already left the wrapped test on the sink counter so she wouldn't have to rummage through the cabinet while needing to pee. She still hopped from foot to foot while she tore it open.

Before the suggested five-minute wait time was up, one very solitary and very solid pink line showed that this month Molly was not pregnant, yet again. She closed her eyes and shook her head, defeated. Then she crawled back into bed and cuddled up to Scott, who was still sleeping, unknowing. She'd tell him over breakfast.

***

THREE HOURS LATER, Molly was packing a red canvas wagon full of the newly potted succulents, milkweed plants, bags of their in-house compost, and veggie seedlings, as well as her vinegar-based weed killer. This nontoxic weed killer didn't affect bees, butterflies, and other beneficial bugs but was lethal to dandelions and other uninvited plants. None of these products were exactly normal Farmer's Market fare, but the town held the event in the Patty's Plant Place parking lot, so they took advantage of the foot traffic. The shop and parking lot were buzzing long before shoppers arrived. Theo had already set up their tent and folding table. Always the helper, he was unloading bins of produce, art, and products for farmers, artisans, bakers, and crafters who were setting up their own booths. May had brought her entire family this week. Her daughter, Hannah, was with Molly in the shop, loading the wagon with their cashbox, flyers, a tablecloth, and other Farmer's Market accessories. Molly loved Hannah's company, especially because of her constant and contagious smile. May, carrying her clipboard, was chatting and checking in both Farmer's Market vendors and the entertainer of the week: a balloon animal twister. Joe and Noah were to be the shopkeepers during the market, and Joe was reacquainting himself with the register and current sales. Noah felt very important to be in charge of the shop, but he was mostly playing with the cat. He had just finished kindergarten and probably would not be quite as much help as Hannah, who had just finished second grade.

Molly took a few minutes to visit the different tables and tents to say hello to the market vendors, following her sister's example. The vendors rewarded her friendliness with samples of cookies, a complimentary box of raspberries, and a bonus bag of hydroponically grown lettuce.

The shop shared its large parking lot with the Buckeye Trail. Patty's Plant Place sat asymmetrically in the parking lot, as if someone had planted it to the side of a flowerpot with most of the parking bays along the side of the store and in front of the trailhead. The Buckeye Trail's blue sign complimented the garden center's yellow-and-blue signage. Molly and May had changed their logo and sign a few years ago so that the "Patty" of Patty's Plant Place wasn't as large as the other text, but new customers still frequently assumed Molly or May were named Patty. On the opposite side of the garden center from the trail was a plaza with Glenn's hiking store, a pharmacy, and a café that was only open for breakfast and lunch. Across the street was the entrance to a housing development. Downtown Hawthorn Heights, farther down the main road, had more storefronts that included a barbershop, an ice cream shop, and the local bank. Municipal buildings, a quaint church, and the elementary school were at the end of town. And so the Farmer's Market was held in both the Patty's Plant Place lot and the Buckeye Trail parking lot.

Returning to the Patty's Plant Place tent, Molly shared her cookies and berries with Hannah. Once customers started trickling into the farmer's market, Hannah accepted five-dollar bills with enthusiasm in exchange for the succulent pots. Molly wondered how her niece was so naturally talkative and friendly to customers. Unless the customer was a regular that she knew personally, Molly often had a hard time finding fodder for small talk.

Their tomato plants sold out first. Molly was glad that she'd grown extra succulents that week and made a note about trying to prepare more tomatoes for the next sale.

A face appeared in the crowd, one that was familiar, yet didn't belong. Molly racked her brain to recognize the man's short hair and brown eyes. He smiled at her, and Molly realized it was Craig, Claudia's new love interest whom she had just met two days before. She smiled back at him.

"Welcome to the Hawthorn Heights Farmer's Market, Craig."

"Hey, Molly. This market certainly is a busy place." Craig held up a bag of Swiss chard, a bundle of basil, and three enormous bulbs of garlic. "I scored on some fresh produce. What do you recommend from your tent here?" He ran his eyes over the display on their table.

"We just ran out of tomato plants, but we've still got cucumber and zucchini plants. You mentioned a garden, but were you planning on growing your own food?" She showed off her gardening supplies and succulents. Craig finally settled on a little jade plant in a white pot, declining the veggie plants. Everyone always wanted succulents.

"I think I'll give it to Claudia. She's going to be mad at me for not inviting her to this outing."

"I'm sure she will." Molly laughed knowingly.

"We also have sales going on in the shop, if you want to go inside. And you can meet the shop cat, Sherlock," Hannah told Craig.

"Oh, Craig, this is my niece, Hannah. Her brother and dad are in the shop for us this morning. My sister and I run the store together. She's over there—May," Molly told him, nodding to her twin, who stood next to the bakery tent.

"A family affair. That's great. I forgot you were a twin, Molly," Craig said.

"We may look alike, but our minds work differently. May is the numbers person, and I know the flowers and growing side of things. She makes the money deliveries, and I deliver the flower arrangements." Hannah laughed at Molly's joke.

"Oh, in that van, huh?" Craig asked, looking over her shoulder and past most of the bustle of the market to the side of the building where the Patty's Plant Place van sat.

"Yep. That's our van. We don't make that many deliveries, honestly," she admitted. "I usually just drive it to and from work."

"A perk of owning your own garden center, huh?" Craig smiled. "Well, thank you for the invitation to shop in the store, Hannah, but I think I'm going to grab a loaf of bread from that bakery tent and get going. It was very nice to meet you."

Hannah extended her hand and said, "It was a pleasure to meet you as well," as she shook Craig's hand. What a polite young lady. Molly would have to tell May about her daughter's good manners.

A few minutes later, Harriett visited the Patty's Plant Place table.

"Harriett, I don't usually see you at the Farmer's Market. You're not here for more vinegar weed killer, are you?" Molly asked, laughing as she greeted her elderly garden center regular.

"Sweetie, I'm here to make sure all of you are alright." She eyed Hannah and lowered her voice conspiratorially, as if the little girl couldn't hear her. "I heard about the missing boy who visited the garden center."

"Oh, yes. The hiker," Molly stammered. No one had actually mentioned Trevor yet that morning. The topic jarred her out of the sunny, celebratory vibe of the market.

"It's just awful. I know how important your customers are to you and May. How attached you get. Just like your dear grandma and grandpa. I knew you would all be worried about the young man."

"It really is horrible. You're right," Molly found herself saying.

"And so I realized that I've never actually made you girls or Theo a batch of my lavender lemon cookies," Harriett continued. "Your Grandma Patty sold me my lavender plant years ago. The lavender lady has thrived so well in my back garden. These cookies are just what you need when worry sets in. They're the scent and taste of calm, I say." Harriett fished a plastic container out of her tote bag that was smooshed full of cookies and placed it on the table in front of Molly. She patted the top of it and continued, "I can pick up the container next time I'm in the shop." Looking around the Farmer's Market, straining her neck, she said, "You'll have to tell me where Theo is. I can't seem to find him in the crowd. I see May over there."

"You are so thoughtful," Molly said, standing. She walked around the table to hug the older woman.

"Well, sweetie, it's just what I do when bad things happen. I make cookies. I say, when life gives you lemons, mix them with lavender!" She rubbed Molly's back during the long hug.

"Harriett, you are wonderful, just wonderful," Molly said, pulling away. The negative pregnancy test, Trevor's disappearance, not knowing where Shannon was, and all the worry that came with it all felt more manageable when people she loved supported her.

The rest of the morning went quickly, with many shoppers requesting tomato plants. Molly thought she might have to order some from a wholesale vendor to keep up with demand.

Once all the sellers and buyers of art, baked goods, pantry goodies, and produce had left, Molly and Hannah repacked the wagon and unloaded it in the store. It was much lighter this time, as they had sold out of nearly everything. Theo pulled the election-style signs out of the grassy buffer strip between the road and their parking lot that advertised the Farmer's Market. May announced that the balloon animal twister was by far the most popular entertainer they had hired.

There were only four bags of compost left after the market, but the display on the shop floor was full. Molly hauled them into the stockroom before heading home. After she finished shoving them onto the shelf, she wiped her hands on her jeans, satisfied with a good day's work—even if it was just half a day. She dug into her pocket for her lip balm and dropped it onto the floor, where it rolled right under a shelf.

On her hands and knees, Molly tried reaching under the shelving unit, but it was farther than her arm would reach. She pulled her phone out of her pocket and shone the flashlight under the shelf. The amount of dust and grime there amazed Molly. She saw the lip balm and something else in the corner. She squeezed between the shelves and the stockroom wall so she could change the angle of retrieval. Molly got her cylinder of lip balm and put it right back in her pocket, dry lips forgotten. Her fingers could just reach the tip of something flat against the wall, maybe a box.

She pulled herself upright, kneeling and looking around for something to extend her reach. The toolbox was on the shelf right in front of her, and she selected a flathead screwdriver. She thought it was probably Grandpa Will's, since it had a wooden handle. So many things of theirs had been left in this shop. The screwdriver was all she needed. She shimmied the box toward her, coughing because of all the dust that she had disturbed. Molly stood up with her treasure, leaving the screwdriver on the floor. It was indeed an old cigar box. The lettering on the side was faded, and the seams were cracked—and it was very heavy for its size. Her breath caught in her throat as she flipped open the lid.

Keys. Dozens of worn, tarnished keys filled the box.

"What's that you have there?" May asked, startling Molly so much that she almost dropped the heavy box.

11

KEYS AND QUESTIONS

"Geesh, you scared me!" Molly yelled, giving May a shove on the shoulder.

"Well, I didn't mean to. I was just trying to find you to say goodbye. But what is this?" May asked, her eyes dropping to the open box in Molly's hands. She poked her finger into the box and turned over the contents.

"I don't know. I just found this box under the shelf a minute ago. It was way in the back." Molly lifted the box in the direction of the shelf to indicate it. Then she selected a key to inspect more closely. It was the largest one she could see and had an ornate head with scrollwork and a bird etched into the metal.

"There are so many of them," May said, and also took a key to examine herself. It looked older than the one in Molly's hand. This one was more like what the twins would have called a "skeleton key." It was longer, with a simpler, round head and a much less complicated but larger bit that would go into the lock itself.

Unplanned and in unison the twins both said, "They must have been Grandma and Grandpa's." Neither giggled this time, but they looked up from their keys to glance at each other.

"There are too many to belong to locks in the store, though," Molly said, looking around as if she could see the entire shop.

"And it's not like the building is a hundred years old or something," May said. "Some of these look really, really old. Like they are from the American Civil War in the 1860s."

"But where could—" Molly started.

"Mo-om," called Noah from the front of the shop.

"Back here!" May yelled back to him. She gave Molly a sheepish smile. "It really is time to head out," she said. "Baseball game later today, you know. Were you guys going to go?"

"We were planning on it. I guess we need to dig into these keys more on Monday morning," Molly said.

"First thing Monday morning. They are just fascinating," May agreed.

"I'll put them on the shelf under the counter in the front. We won't miss them that way."

"I don't know. I don't want Aiden to get into

them," May said, making a worried face. Aiden was another high school student who worked nights and weekends. He had arrived at 12:30 and would close the shop up at 9:00 p.m. with Ryan. Aiden had sandy hair and braces and was not nearly as responsible as Charlotte. He frequently got bored and did unexpected things that he thought were helpful—but just weren't. One time, he stacked bags of fertilizer to the ceiling. But only fertilizer. He left plenty of other items unstocked that night.

"Okay. Let's leave them back here," Molly said, looking around.

"Are you ladies ready to leave?" Joe asked from the doorway. Both Molly and May jumped. Molly almost dropped the box filled with keys for a second time.

This key box made Molly so skittish. She felt like everyone walked in so suddenly when she was holding it.

"We are. Just need to put this away," May said. She took the box from Molly and closed the lid in one movement. She placed it quickly on a stock shelf, on top of a box of trowels at shoulder height. Aiden probably wouldn't look there. Molly wondered if May was trying to keep the box from Joe. She'd certainly be telling Scott all about her find when she got home.

"The kids are hungry," Joe told them. "We need to get some food in them before the game, more than just cookies. It's been a fun morning, though. I'd like to come to the Farmer's Market more often."

"I'm glad you were here, Joe," Molly said with a smile. "Thanks for your help."

"I don't think we received the evidence you were going to drop off yesterday, Molly. I meant to ask you about it earlier," Joe said, giving Molly his full attention and rocking on the balls of his toes.

"I know. I'm just not sure it has anything to do with the investigation. It's probably Shannon's earring, but I haven't heard from her, and I don't want to turn it in if she is also missing."

"You didn't tell me that," May said, her voice higher than normal. "I thought you were just turning it in. Shannon never responds to us quickly. I'm sure she's just fine." Molly knew she was hurt. She hadn't actually told May about the text with the picture she sent Shannon yet—and that she still hadn't gotten a response. Usually, she told her twin about nearly everything that happened in her life, and she got the same updates from May in return.

"Well, I really think it's hers, and it wasn't close to the ... well, to the bridge where they think Trevor was last. And I texted her without thinking. I asked Shannon if the earring was hers directly. Well, in a text. But I asked her, so now I won't be anonymously turning it into the police. She'd know it was me. And I'm worried about her."

"Ugh! She's the worst!" May rolled her eyes and

made a disgusted face. "She'll lie about it if she thinks it has anything to do with the police. You can never really believe anything Shannon says, anyway. We'll never really know now."

"Well, I didn't want to just turn it in without telling her I found it. It felt wrong. Like I was lying to her," Molly retorted. "If she's not missing herself."

"Who cares!" May put her hands on her hips, and her eyes drilled into Molly's. May was really reacting strongly to all of this.

"We don't know if it has anything to do with the case," Joe put in, and laid a hand on the back of his wife's shoulder to help calm her. "The earring wasn't at the scene itself, just nearby. I think Molly should decide what she wants to do with it. I do think we need to try to discover Shannon's whereabouts, however."

"I'll drive past her house again. What I really want to do is figure out if the earring is actually Shannon's, figure out if she was on the trail, figure out if she was on the trail at the same time as Trevor, figure out what she was doing on the trail, and figure out if she's missing or not. There's a lot to figure out, and I don't know how to do it," Molly said.

12

TOO MUCH EYE CONTACT AND GOOD COP/ BAD COP

Molly ignored the texts from Archie that she received Saturday morning during the Farmer's Market. She just texted him, "Sorry—busy day" while she was at the baseball game, sitting in lawn chairs in the shade between May and Scott. He asked twice via text if she wanted to "grab dinner" with him, but she didn't respond. Admittedly, she spent some time texting with Claudia about her worry about Shannon and the found earring when she should have been cheering on Noah. She also told her friend about the negative pregnancy test, and Claudia commiserated with her.

Also during the game, Molly texted Shannon, asking if her boss had liked the coneflowers. There was only so much she could think of to say to Shannon. Still no response. Maybe Shannon had just misplaced her phone.

Noah's team won the game and were all going out for ice cream to celebrate.

When she and Scott were getting in his car, she got another text from Archie and muttered under her breath, "So persistent!" This time, he even asked if Scott wanted to go, too.

"Who's persistent?" Scott asked.

"Oh, Archie. He's still in town and keeps asking if I want to go to dinner." Scott snorted. "I haven't really responded, and I do *not* want to have dinner with him. Like, at all. But he asked if you wanted to go this time. Persistent!"

"Oh, I'm invited?" Scott perked up, interested. "Where did he want to go to dinner? What about sushi?"

"Scott! Why would we go out to dinner with him? He's unbearably talkative."

"But I can always go for sushi."

"He didn't actually say sushi. We could really just go on our own!" she told him, exasperated.

"So you've mentioned that this guy is being flirty? Can't do that with me there. If he does, I promise, I'll hit him." Molly rolled her eyes and Scott laughed, confirming that he was not serious about the physical violence. "But you said that he's also being secretive while being so chatty-chatty. You want to get some answers about those boots and where he was when Trevor went missing, right?"

"I do," Molly said thoughtfully. "But do you really want to go out to dinner with Archie?"

"Seems that I should meet the guy," Scott said, straightening his shoulders. "Set him straight. Find out about the boots. We can work together to figure it out. I don't really want to hang out with him all night. Dinner seems like the perfect place to talk."

"Scott, there's really nothing he actually did to flirt with me. He just gave me a weird vibe in person compared to over email. You don't need to say anything to him. I can take care of myself, and I do not want to have dinner with him. You really don't need to threaten him." She buckled her seatbelt and felt like the conversation was over.

Scott didn't let the conversation die, though. "You know I wouldn't actually ever hit him. And I won't say anything. I'll set him straight *with my eyes*. I'll put my arm around you and make too much eye contact. Like, an uncomfortable amount of eye contact. It's guy code. He'll understand without words."

Molly laughed. "Oh, my goodness! You are so ridiculous!"

"Right? That's why you love me." And Scott buckled his seatbelt and started the car.

"I do. I really do love you, Scotty. But I don't want to eat dinner with Archie."

"We can go to the quick sushi place. And I can be

a steamroller. I'll be a steamroller talker." Scott made a slicing motion with his hand and a noise with his mouth that Molly assumed he thought was a steamroller. She didn't understand how the slicing motion had anything to do with a steamroller but let it pass.

"Scott ..." Molly said, not even sure how to respond, but he rambled on, adamant.

"I just don't like the weird vibe. I've always felt uncomfortable about him. You know that. I just want to meet him and show off that we're happy and he has no right to flirt with you, even if he's not. And talk about his boots."

Molly threw up her hands. "Fine. We'll meet him for sushi." She knew that if she didn't agree, Scott wouldn't let it go for the rest of the weekend.

So once again, Molly caved to Scott's stomach. Maybe his heart too. She texted Archie back to say that they would meet up at a Japanese place in downtown Cleveland at 7:00 p.m. At least then the text barrage would stop. For that alone, she felt a bit relieved.

"Before we go home, I really want to stop by Shannon's house again. I'm worried about her," Molly said.

"Yeah. Okay," Scott agreed. "It is kinda weird that she hasn't responded at all. Let's see what we can see."

Molly was thankful that Scott wasn't blowing off her concern for Shannon like May was. They pulled onto Shannon's street and saw Shannon's white SUV pulling out of her driveway.

"There she is! There she is!" Molly shouted, and grabbed Scott's shoulder, shaking it.

"Hey now! Don't distract the driver," Scott said. "Seems she's not missing. That's reassuring."

"Yeah, just ignoring me, as usual." Molly stared at her cousin in the SUV as they passed by. "With a ponytail and that hot pink workout shirt, it looks like she's going to the gym."

"Well, that mystery is solved, at least. Still no answer on if it's her earring, though."

"I'm just relieved to know that whatever happened to Trevor didn't happen to Shannon too." Molly blew out a deep breath and patted Scott's shoulder where she'd shaken it. "Thanks for helping me figure out that she's okay."

"I've always got your back, Molly. You know that."

* * *

AND SO MOLLY was eating out for the third time in as many days and a second time with Archie, even though she had promised herself she wouldn't see him again during his visit to Ohio. This time, though, she had Scott, who would help even out Archie's tendency to take over any conversation.

She and Scott arrived early, and a waiter seated them at a table where they could watch the sushi chefs, the *itamae*, do their delicate job of crafting, rolling, and cutting sushi. After ordering drinks, Scott visited the sushi chefs to ask for recommendations and watch them work. Molly felt much more comfortable at this restaurant than she had the previous day at Greensward. She knew the place and the menu. Also, she came prepared with a second layer to combat too cold summer air-conditioning. Scott could fill some of the voids of idle conversation, and they were unified in trying to ask about Archie's boots.

Molly was glad that Scott also felt suspicious of her editor. It was just so uncanny that he arrived at the same time as the police after Brooks had raised the alarm about Trevor. She thought about mentioning this oddity to Joe, but she had nothing of substance to tell him. Some muddy boots and an inconveniently timed entry weren't much to go on. At least with Shannon's earring, there was physical evidence. Plus, Archie was sort of her boss. She certainly didn't want to get on his bad side. But if he'd done something to Trevor, he needed to be brought to justice. She considered again why she wanted to sort out this mystery. She didn't know who to voice her concerns to, and they just didn't seem to be big enough concerns to bother anyone with them. But she felt responsible for the sweet hiker, and she would do what she could to see if Archie or Shannon had anything to do with his disappearance.

As Scott was returning to their table, Molly texted Claudia about the dinner with Archie and their plans to talk with him about his muddy boots. Claudia wished her good luck and yummy sushi.

"So, listen," Scott said as he sat down. "I think we need a plan of attack. I'm not here to be Archie's friend. I'm glad you do these articles for his magazine. It brings the shop some notoriety, and it's cool work. Some extra money in the winter when the shop is mostly closed in January and February. But I don't like that he's so friendly. I'm not here to become his chum."

"Sure, I know," Molly told him, wondering where he was going with this little speech. She shifted in her seat.

"I'm here to meet this guy who's hitting on my wife. Stand up for her." Molly started to interject, but he continued. Or, perhaps, steamrolled her. "I know you can stand on your own. But I'm here to be proof of life—proof that you're not available. We're happily married. There's no reason you'd fall into his arms." Scott paused and nodded his head for emphasis as he continued. "And I'm here to talk about Trevor."

"Right. Me too." Molly sat up a little straighter. "I already said I wouldn't want to be around this guy a second time this weekend, if not for Trevor."

"Right. So I think I should be the jerk. I'll steamroll him like I said, and I'm not going to go out of my way to be polite. You ask nicely. I'll be more direct where you just—aren't." Molly started to interrupt him again. "You're too nice to people you don't know well. Or most people, really. I know you. So I'll be the bad cop, and you can be the good cop. You stay on his good side so you don't get fired. I don't care what he thinks about me when this dinner is over."

Molly wanted to respond, but just as Scott finished his sentence, they saw the hostess guiding Archie across the restaurant to their table. He was wearing his hiking boots.

13

MISO SOUP AND BLUE BLAZES

"Scott! It's so good to meet you!" Archie nearly yelled and shook Scott's hand with so much enthusiasm that Molly had to actively make sure she wasn't cringing. She looked around, and, indeed, some people were staring at their table.

"Yeah, real good to meet you too," Scott said in a much quieter tone. He quickly sat down and spent too much time pulling in his chair.

"So you guys are sushi people?" Archie asked as he sat down and picked up the menu.

"Yes, we certainly are." Molly took the lead on sweet chitchat to let Scott recover from the showy greeting.

"So, what's your favorite thing here?" Archie asked as he studied the menu intently. Again, he fiddled with the metal corner of the menu and became quiet.

Scott told Archie that he had just discussed the day's specials and favorites with the *itamae*. He was planning on ordering *ebi nigiri*, or cooked shrimp over sushi rice, as well as the sweet potato maki rolls. The waiter served them each complimentary salad and miso soup. Archie was characteristically enthusiastic and rambling.

"I've never had sweet potato sushi. I just stick to the lazy American avocado or California rolls. And are California rolls really Japanese, or are they from California? Probably not from Japan, right? I'm so glad you asked for recommendations. This is going to be delicious! Thanks for inviting me!"

Molly almost laughed out loud. The man sounded like an excited seven-year-old. And had she really invited him? She thought not. Scott looked at her, his wide eyes affirming her assessment of the situation.

Archie gave the menu his full attention until the waiter returned to take their order, but ordered the same thing Scott did despite his deep studying. He seemed to trust Scott's advice.

"So, how was the Home and Garden Show today?" Molly knew it would be a good opening question.

"Wonderful! I talked to about thirty vendors that I didn't get to during my time at the show yesterday. I know it's not the ideal time to decide on or select new partners during a busy show like this, but it's all about the leads. I was especially excited about a recycled content trellis I thought you would also be interested in, knowing your enthusiasm for environmental efforts. The vendor has one made of sturdy recycled plastic and one made of metal as well. I was wondering if you'd want to write up a comparison. Perhaps you could report on which is better for specific plants? I'm not quite sure yet if that's what I want you to focus on next, but I'll let you know." Molly found that she was mindlessly nodding during his monologue.

Molly felt like she interrupted Archie when she said, "You'll have to send me the details."

"I will when I return to the office in a few days. It will take me nearly a week to wade through all my notes and organize all the new information while I'm also editing content for the next magazine. Home and Garden Shows take a lot of work on the back end."

"Sure, take your time," Molly told him and then looked over at Scott, passing the baton with a glance.

"Molly said you were interested in hiking on our Buckeye Trail." Scott spoke quickly so that Archie wouldn't start up again.

"I had intentions of hiking the trail that first night I was in Ohio, but with all the activity at the garden center with the police, I didn't think it was in good taste to just head off onto the trail where a young man went missing and possibly got hurt." He looked down at his silverware and chopsticks and arranged them into a straight line.

"You didn't hike before you came to the shop, then?" Molly asked without thinking. Was this being a good cop? She wasn't sure, but she was going to take the opportunity to ask the question. "I thought you did. Weren't your boots muddy before you got there?"

The waiter came back and removed the salad plates. Scott raised his eyebrows across the table at Molly. Would they get their answer before they even got dinner?

"No, I didn't get on the trail before I got to the shop." Archie seemed downright mopey. He hadn't been on the trail! It was so easy to get an answer out of him this time.

"Well, maybe you can get out there tomorrow. When are you leaving?" Scott asked and then slurped up some soup.

"I'm leaving early Monday morning and will take a couple of days off from work when I return to Boston. Perhaps I could find some time tomorrow afternoon when I'm done at the show. The thing is, it's always so exhausting talking to people all day and walking around at any Home and Garden Show. There's so much to see, and although I do wear quality shoes, my feet are always beat by the end of the day."

"It is really hard to be on your feet all day and to talk to people all day. I agree," Molly said between spoonfuls of soup. He still hadn't told them about his boots, and she wanted to steer him back in that direction.

"Yes. It's worth it, though," Archie said with a sigh. He had more to say on the subject, for sure, and had his mouth open to continue.

Scott spoke quickly, before Archie could get more words out. "Molly and I like to go hiking on the trail together. We have matching headlamps."

Molly knew that this was Scott's attempt to prove they had a happy marriage, since they were not sitting next to each other. Molly was glad for the square tables at this restaurant instead of booths that had conveniently spoiled Scott's ridiculous plan of having his arm wrapped around her while he stared Archie down. But the conversation was not going where she wanted. She needed to know about those muddy boots. She was also glad that he wasn't being flirty in this setting and wasn't sure if it was Scott's presence or not. Perhaps she was just not used to his talkative ways.

"We used them yesterday, actually. Was it just yesterday? We were on the trail before breakfast." And the idea came to her. "Maybe you could try going out before the show starts tomorrow morning?

Before your feet get tired and you're exhausted from the busy day."

"That's a wonderful idea! My feet wouldn't hurt in the morning. Tomorrow is the last day I'll be going to the show, so maybe I can get a little worn out before I hit the vendors. But will I need a headlamp —or at least a flashlight—like you use?"

There was no way Molly was going to lend her headlamp to Archie. Scott must have been thinking the same thing because he said, "The sun is up by six thirty at this time of year. It is darker under the trees, but if you're out there by seven or so, you won't need a lamp. We rarely use them much in the summer. They're usually a trail tool we use in the spring or in the fall, after the time change."

"Right," Molly murmured in agreement.

"Okay, good. I don't think that I'd really go that early, anyway. I like to have something in my stomach before I leave for the day. This is great. I'll finally go hiking during my visit to Ohio! I really should find a trail in Boston I like too. Would you two want to be my guides on the Buckeye Trail?" He asked, his eyes shifting from Molly to Scott and back.

Molly felt like a deer caught in the headlights. Scott cleared his throat and said, "There's an app you should download. Guthook, I think it's called? It's actually rather hard to get off the trail. They have blue lines painted on trees all along it. The blue blazes." Was this Scott being the bad cop? He certainly wasn't steamrolling anyone.

"Oh, I do like a good map app," Archie said, putting down his spoon to dig into his pocket.

"But this won't be your first time hiking in your boots, right? I think they were muddy when I met you the other day, weren't they?" Molly threw out this short string of unrelated questions as casually as she could. Archie had already pulled his phone out and was searching for the app Scott had mentioned.

"Oh, I do get on some trails at the Breakheart Reservation north of Boston once in a while, but that's the only place I've ever been. I really want to hike more," Archie said slowly and succinctly, distracted by his phone, the blue light reflecting on his face.

Molly smiled at Scott, who took her hand and placed it on the table under his. She knew he'd try to make eye contact with Archie next. Now he didn't have to get mean about asking Archie pointed questions about his muddy boots and hiking on the Buckeye Trail at the same time as Trevor. She had asked the questions herself.

14

THE SUCCULENT SLEUTH AND MORNING PLANS

"Honestly, I don't know why I ever thought Archie could have hurt someone," Molly told Claudia later that night on the phone while waving her arms around and pacing the living room, talking at nearly Archie's fast pace. "I mean, he's not a totally normal guy. He's really, really talkative. He stands too close. He's too friendly and excitable. He's kind of weird. But I don't think he'd hurt Trevor. I feel so good knowing that he wasn't on the trail that day. He wants to be a hiker, but he's not. Not yet."

Molly and Scott's living room was decorated in warm, natural tones. The brown leather sofa held soft, lime-colored pillows. A huge snake plant dominated one corner of the room beside the television stand. An arrowhead plant draped over the picture window, from which Molly had produced more offspring via cuttings to hand off to friends and family than she could count. Their home wasn't the largest in the neighborhood, but it was cozy and filled with greenery.

"You did it, Molls! You're a downright detective ... You're ... you're the succulent sleuth!" Claudia announced.

"Well, I don't know about that. And really? The 'succulent sleuth'? Why always with the succulents?" Molly waved her arms around for emphasis, even though Claudia couldn't see her. Scott walked across the room and grinned at her, waving his arms around mockingly.

"I think it sounds cute. And you totally asked the right questions, got to the bottom of it. Like a sleuth boss!"

"Got to the bottom of one possible not-so-much-of-a-suspect. The police didn't consider him a suspect at all." Molly paused. "I feel pretty fantastic about it, though," she conceded, smiling widely.

"Well, I don't think that they really knew when Archie got to the shop or that he acted like he really wanted to go hiking that day. It was fishy, and you saw that. I think you were right to follow up with some ... investigation, some sleuthing," Claudia said, laughing.

"It was fishy. But he didn't do it. And Trevor is still missing." The tone of the conversation cooled.

"It is really frustrating that they haven't found

him at all yet," Claudia agreed. "Craig said he saw the police were doing something downstream in the river under the Oakway Bridge, even farther down the trail."

"Oh, man," Molly said. "That means they're searching for his body if they're looking in the water. I really keep hoping that he's okay, just missing."

"I don't know. It's been days at this point. You can't really be missing for days and be okay. We might need to face facts here, friend."

"He was just such a sweet guy. So funny and friendly. So excited to be hiking, so excited for the future." Molly's voice cracked. She sat down on the sofa and hugged a green pillow. Claudia made empathetic noises. "He might be in the woods with two broken legs, existing on acorns and rain water. Maybe?"

"Let's not focus on the sad stuff." Claudia paused. "You ruled out one suspect. You're fighting for him. And you've got the earring lead. Shannon is not missing. Which is good, but she's still suspicious. There's more to do. And I want to help. What's your next step?" Claudia was always so full of resolve and positivity.

Molly rubbed her face and sniffed. "I'm sure the detectives are doing what they can do. It's their job. But yeah, they don't know about this earring. I just feel so bad about turning it in. It might be Shannon's, but it might not be. I need to ask her more directly." She paused. "I'll do it tomorrow."

"Tomorrow is good. But what about if you prepared for it? Like, wrote down what you wanted to say to Shannon?"

Molly laughed. "Oh, you know me so well. You're right. I should have a script. That would work better. Do you think you could help me figure out what I should say?"

Molly went into the kitchen and sat down at the table, where she wrote down some ideas and eventually, with Claudia's help, some full sentences. Claudia was an excellent coach, as she was much more direct than Molly would ever be. Scott hovered a bit and made a bowl of popcorn during the brainstorming session.

Once they finished Molly's script for talking to Shannon, Molly announced, "I'm also thinking that I want to go see the bridge myself." She chewed on the pen cap.

"See the scene of the crime," Claudia said in an agreeable tone.

"Did you see the picture they released in the newspaper? I saw it online, and I don't think it was a recent picture, like since it happened. I think the picture is even from a different year because it's not the right season."

"Oh, that's shady."

"Well, I don't think it's really shady. They just

didn't have a current photo. But the wildflowers that were in bloom in the picture were wrong for this time of year."

"You and flowers. You really make a good detective."

"I guess plants just speak to me," Molly told Claudia. "Anyway, as of this morning, there was still police tape blocking off the trailhead on that side. And I don't know what the bridge looks like now. I want to know."

"So ... you're going to bust down the tape and march right down the trail to see what's what?"

"I was thinking of gingerly crawling under the tape, *Mission Impossible* style, and quietly tiptoeing down the trail in the dark." Molly laughed at their contrasting perspectives.

"That sounds more your style," Claudia chuckled. "So that's how I'll help. I'll hold the tape up for you and tiptoe down the trail by your side, real quiet. Call me Dr. Claudia Watson."

"You're sure about this? I don't know what happens when you trespass beyond police tape. I don't know what kind of trouble you get into."

"I guess you could bring someone else, but I'm the first to volunteer here, Molls. Don't look a gift donkey up the butt, or whatever."

It took Molly a full minute to recover from laughing. "It's a gift horse in the mouth, not a donkey! Donkey? Up the butt? Oh, my goodness! Oh, my."

Claudia was laughing too. "Anyway, okay." Molly recovered with a couple of slow breaths. "I want to go, but I'm nervous about it. Maybe we should do some planning. What do we need? When should we go?"

"What's the matter with tomorrow morning? What is there to plan? We'll just bring some flashlights. Maybe you should drive Scott's car instead of the garden center van with your big blue and yellow logo on the side. Or we park down the road or something. Doesn't seem so complicated," Claudia said, always ready to act.

"Yeah. Okay." Molly was not so ready.

"Don't lose your momentum here. There's not anything else to think about. And we'll just take a look. We won't be there long and won't mess anything up. I'm sure we won't even be the first people to do it. It's public property, hard to lock down."

"All compelling arguments. I guess you're right," Molly agreed. And so they made plans to meet at the neighboring plaza at 4:30 a.m., well before daylight.

15

ANOTHER HIKE IN THE DARK AND A MYSTERIOUS PERSON

Sunday morning, before daylight hit the canopy of trees along the Buckeye Trail, Claudia and Molly were both psyching each other up to breach the police tape of a crime scene. Molly had prepared travel mugs of her favorite coffee with chocolate chips and a splash of cream for both of them. Scott had woken up long enough to wish her well and to say he would make the coffee but had fallen back to sleep before he even made it out of bed.

Molly and Claudia chatted excitedly as they walked from the plaza parking lot with the hiking store, pharmacy, and café where they'd left their cars. Claudia played clarinet in the community band and was looking forward to her next concert the following weekend. Although she had been insistent the night before, Claudia was more hesitant when it came down to probably breaking the law. Molly hadn't thought of this location as a crime scene yet and said as much.

"Me too. It's just such a normal place for us," Claudia thought out loud. "It's weird that something bad happened, and it makes it less normal. Now it's a more important place, a place that means more to other people. A place with more consequence. Not just a trail now."

"And we could normally just go for a walk in the woods any time of the day we wanted, but now we have to sneak around in the dark."

"Right. I'm not normally nervous about going on a hike," Claudia agreed.

They had arrived at the blocked-off trailhead. Only one car was in the parking lot: an older navy blue Ford. It seemed familiar, but Molly couldn't place it.

"I think we just need to rip off the band-aid. Are you ready, my gift donkey?" Molly asked Claudia, taking her friend's arm in her own.

Claudia laughed and replied, "Ready if you are, succulent sleuth."

"Let's make sure these aren't new nicknames that stick after this probably illegal hike."

They gingerly nudged the police tape out of their way in just two places and replaced it. Molly noted that it was more beat up than she could see from her vantage from the Patty's Plant Place window. The wind had creased the yellow plastic, and the early summer sun had already discolored the yellow where it folded on itself. Tree limbs tattered some of the tape's edges. Other visitors—perhaps not only the police, as Claudia surmised—had definitely moved it and replaced the tape more than a few times in multiple places.

As they moved from the well-lit parking lot into the trail, the light diminished quickly. Just a few minutes in, the trail was deeply dark. Moonlight and starlight did not penetrate the tree canopy. Molly turned on her headlamp, and Claudia clicked her flashlight to life, but kept them aimed only toward the trail to stay stealthy. A blanket of quiet lay over the entire forest, at first. But the farther they walked, the more noises Molly's ears picked up. She knew nocturnal animals would still be awake, but she didn't see any eyes reflecting light through the dark. Songbirds were not awake yet. Dew had formed already and glimmered from leaves on the ground in their rays of light.

They walked along in silence, an unstated understanding that they were to keep quiet on this mission, although it was very unlikely there would be anyone else around to hear them.

The trail snaked around in the forest, avoiding larger trees and boulders that had existed before the trail itself did. After a few more minutes of walking, they could hear the rushing water of the river that the bridge crossed. It was peaceful to listen to forest noises arising in the dark's coolness. Molly looked over at Claudia and smiled; despite their grim mission, she loved few things more than being on a trail with good company. After a few more minutes, they could see a break in the trees ahead and the stars peeking through. Molly knew they were nearly at the bridge. She wasn't sure what to expect, but knew she wouldn't feel satisfied until she saw it with her own eyes.

At the next twist in the trail, Molly saw how the texture of the bridge and the wooden truss structure above it contrasted with their current crushed limestone path. On the bridge, however, was a surprise. A beam of light shone from a flashlight, and they could see the silhouette of a person who had patches of reflective material on their clothing and their shoes. Molly and Claudia were not alone after all.

Both women stopped in their tracks. Molly thought the person hadn't seen them yet. She motioned for Claudia to get off the trail, and they both high-stepped into the woods, turning their lights off.

"Who is that?" Claudia hissed.

"Someone else is here!" Molly whispered at the same time. Molly worried that their rushed exit and whispering were too loud and had alerted the person to their presence.

Wide-eyed, heart thumping, Molly whispered,

"Of course, whoever that is has no reason to be on the trail at this time of day except to inspect the bridge—just like us."

"Totally agree," Claudia said quietly, craning her neck to look at the bridge through the trees.

"What do we do?" Molly wanted to hide from the person and confront them at the same time.

"I say we sneak up on them and see if they are trying to change the scene of the crime."

"Oh, my goodness! You don't think it's the person who hurt Trevor, do you?" Molly had just thought it was someone being nosy, not the person who should be in jail.

"I don't know, but sneaking around in the dark isn't a totally innocent thing to do. I know we are, but you're involved in the case."

"I'm definitely not involved in the case in any official way. I was just questioned by the police." She considered a moment. "So, do you want to ask them what they're doing or just see what they're doing? Do we talk to them, or do we stalk them?" Molly didn't know what she wanted to do, but she sure wanted to get closer.

"Him. I think it's a dude. I say we get closer and see if he runs away or not. We can talk if he lets us. I think he'd only talk if he's innocent, though, right?" Claudia always sounded so sure of herself.

"I mean, I think that if someone had tried to talk to us right now, I might try to run away too, and we're innocent." Then Molly added, "We're innocent of hurting anyone, but maybe not innocent of trespassing."

"Okay, so let's creep over there real quiet. I think we can see him through the trees if we cross the trail and walk on the other side. What do you think?" Claudia asked.

Molly looked around, craning her neck to see the larger picture of the forest around them, and then agreed. They hunched their shoulders and walked on their toes to the edge of the trail. It was slow going without their lights, and they both made more noise than they expected or wanted. At the trail, Molly held her breath and then crossed as quickly and silently as she could. Claudia was right behind her. They were between the river and the Buckeye Trail, where more light reached the forest. That made seeing easier but also meant there was more undergrowth in their way.

They crept along for about one hundred feet, until they could make out the person on the bridge. Now that they weren't scampering into the woods at Usain Bolt speed so they wouldn't be spotted, Molly could see that the figure on the bridge was indeed a man. He was wearing dark clothes but had reflective patches on his shoes and along the sides of his shorts. Molly didn't really expect him to still be there because she thought they'd made so much noise that he would certainly have heard them and dashed away, trying not to be seen himself. But somehow he was still there and hadn't noticed them at all.

After another hundred feet or so, they were close enough to make out the guy's features. Molly stretched out her arm to stop Claudia and then took out her phone and zoomed in on the familiar face to take a picture. It was Brooks Thompson, the runner who had found Trevor's backpack and walking stick. She felt like she needed proof, a pictorial reminder of whom she'd stumbled upon in the woods so early in the morning.

16

A MISSED CONFRONTATION AND A BROKEN BRIDGE

It shocked Molly to see Brooks in the woods before daybreak inspecting the crime scene, the crime scene that he himself alerted the world to, the only crime scene that she had ever really cared much about, and the only crime scene that he and Molly had in common. After staring at him for a moment, she could see that he was wearing white earbuds and probably listening to some running music and had not heard them. Certainly, if he hadn't been, he would have heard their loud entry into the woods for cover.

Molly told Claudia all of this in a whisper. Even though Molly and Claudia had talked about that emotion-heavy afternoon when Brooks arrived at the shop in such a state, Molly hadn't actually given much detail about him.

"So I guess we don't have to whisper so quietly,"

Claudia said to Molly, but still in a hushed voice. "I mean, if it's him, he's on our team, right?" Molly nodded an affirmative, but then shrugged. "But what in the world is he doing here so early in the morning? Not a normal time for a run. I think he's here to look at the crime scene like us."

"I don't know, but I know that I definitely want to go over there and talk to him and see what he's up to. Now that I know that I've met this mystery person, I'm not so freaked out. Super weird that we're here at the same time snooping on the crime scene, right?"

"Do you really think he's going to be so friendly and just chat with us?" Claudia asked. "I'm not so sure that your general trust in people is so applicable at this time of the day in the dark."

"We know each other. I'd talk to him if I met him on the trail." Claudia made an overly dramatic, unbelieving face. "Even at this time of day," Molly reported.

"Well, then, let's go talk to this guy you know so well," Claudia said and started back to the trail before Molly could say anything else. Molly followed her, and they walked the rest of the short distance to the bridge on the trail, limestone crunching under their feet. They turned their lights back on to see the trail more clearly.

The friends were still about twenty feet away from the bridge when Molly yelled a greeting and waved at him. It was then that Brooks noticed the pair for the first time. He seemed to be inspecting every inch of the bridge before he looked up. However, as Claudia expected and to Molly's dismay, when Brooks saw the women approaching, he took off down the trail in the opposite direction and ran away. Molly really wanted to understand what he was doing and wanted to talk to him more the closer they got, but then he disappeared into the dark.

"Well, I guess he didn't want to talk," Claudia quipped to her friend.

"Did he recognize me? Why would he run away from me when he purposely ran to our shop after he called the police? This is just weird." She blew out a long breath. "We'll never catch him." After a beat she added, "I guess we're here to see the bridge anyway, not Brooks."

And so Molly and Claudia finally reached their intended mission point. There were no electric lights on the bridge, but without the tree cover, the space was more illuminated than when they were within the trees. They still kept their lights on.

"What was he looking for?" Claudia asked.

When they stood on the bridge, the damage the structure had sustained shocked Molly. As a truss bridge, it had large, squared-off timbers that made looming triangles on either side of the walkway. The entire thing was painted brown, and the trusses were at least fifteen feet above Molly's head. At elbow height, there were also boards that acted as both a guardrail and a handrail across the entire structure. There were large cracks at many points on the handrails and even the trusses. Molly and Claudia had been on this bridge many times and recognized that this was recent damage.

The largest break point took Molly's breath away. One board of the handrail had ragged edges where it was cracked through and was totally missing between the trusses. Someone could have easily fallen into the river between the missing boards. No wonder they were looking downstream for Trevor's body. What happened here that had damaged the bridge so badly? Did Trevor get mauled by a bear? Maybe a group of many people attacked Trevor?

Molly took some pictures with her phone but knew they wouldn't turn out well. She wished she could see the entire bridge at once instead of bits of it at a time with her headlamp. It was eerie, wondering about past violence committed, without light to illuminate the complete story. Both Claudia and Molly wandered back and forth, exploring the entire bridge. Claudia seemed to have nothing to say, which was a rarity. Molly found the perspective of the photo used in the local newspaper and confirmed that the flowers in the photo were not currently blooming. She didn't blame them for not using a current image of the bridge.

"So, ah, I think there's blood over here. And over

there," Claudia said, breaking the silence and pointing.

"How did I not see it?" Molly stepped over to where Claudia was standing.

"I don't know," Claudia said without humor in her voice. She lit up a portion of one of the upright truss supports with her flashlight. Molly had to tilt her head up to see a splatter of blood.

"Here too," Claudia said simply and took a few steps to cross the bridge and illuminate a crack in the handrail with another dark stain.

"Someone was hurt here," Molly stated, the gravity of it sinking in.

"But look right over here." Claudia pointed with her flashlight again and Molly inspected it with her. "There's another stain here, but I think they tried to clean it up." Indeed, this stain was moved around and smeared, but still present.

"Not very well. But I think you're right. The person who hurt Trevor tried to wipe up some of the blood," Molly thought out loud.

"There are one, two, three, four blood splatters," Claudia stated. "Only one that might have been cleaned up. My guess is, that one is the killer's."

"Who's the detective now? I didn't think of that. Trying to not leave behind DNA evidence." She paused in thought. "I keep hoping there's no killer, but this makes me really think that Trevor is more than just missing."

17

SHANNON'S CALL AND DAYLIGHT

Despite being awake much earlier than normal and with the heavy weight on her heart that came with the visit to the crime scene, Molly was determined to make sure she contacted Shannon and, if her cousin didn't answer her phone, go to her house yet again and wait. She'd promised Claudia that she would.

After returning home, Molly slipped back into bed with Scott and slept in until eight thirty. After some breakfast, she sat on the deck in her reading chair with the notes she and Claudia had made the night before. She had reviewed them five times and knew by heart the points she wanted to make. The rose-gold hoop earring was sitting next to her on the side table. She picked it up and flipped it around, deep in thought. It was only nine thirty. Was that too early to call someone on a Sunday morning? Did

Shannon sleep in like a teenager? Molly didn't know, but she didn't want to put it off any longer. Flattening her lips with determination, she deposited the earring back on the table and tapped Shannon's number on her phone.

It went directly to voicemail.

That was okay. Molly and Claudia had a plan for voicemail. Molly concentrated on not being too chatty and also not allowing her nerves to edge into her voice. She knew what she was going to say this time and had to stay on topic.

"Hey, Shannon. It's Molly. Hope you're having a good weekend. Just wanted to check in about the earring I found. It's really pretty. It looks expensive, and I think it might be yours. And what will I do with just one earring? I might just throw it away if I can't find the owner. Call me when you can."

These were all Claudia's ideas: play to Shannon's ego and compliment the beauty of the piece of jewelry. Threatening to throw away the earring seemed like a good idea to make it more urgent, but very unlike Molly's habits. She'd never throw away something so valuable in the trash. Shannon probably didn't really know that, though. Molly knew the two points were likely to spur her cousin to respond.

She picked up the earring again, stared at it, and willed it to give her new information about where it came from and what it knew. Molly was about to stand up to go over to Shannon's house.

She did not expect Shannon to call her back almost immediately.

"Hello, Molly, I got your voicemail. I am actually missing an earring." Shannon bulldozed over Molly even saying hello. Molly was happier than she had ever been to hear Shannon's voice. She was still relieved that Shannon wasn't missing, but she needed to figure out what was going on with the earring and whether Shannon had something to do with Trevor's last hike on the Buckeye Trail.

"Great! Did you see the picture I texted you? It's a rose-gold hoop that needs an earring back. I didn't find the back, of course. It kind of has a twist to it, two strands looped together like a rope." Molly wasn't keeping to her script anymore; she was too excited that Shannon was claiming the earring as her own.

"Yes, I believe it's mine," Shannon replied, with no friendliness in her voice.

"That's great. I found it the day after you were in the store last time. I found it on Friday morning. You were there Thursday." This was the start of the bait.

"That's fine. Will you have it at the shop tomorrow? I can swing by and get it then." Shannon didn't even respond to the day it went missing. So frustrating!

"I can leave it there. It's at my house now. Did the hoop go missing on Thursday?" Molly picked up the earring again and lined it up so she could see her neighbor's chimney through the hoop. She closed her left eye and mused how the chimney moved. Claudia and Molly's plan was to be as persistent as she had been with Archie to get to the answers. Ask a different way. She was ready to sit for a while and keep asking.

"Actually, yes. I believe I was wearing it when I was at the store, and it went missing then. I recall talking about the pink plant I bought and how tall it would grow." Persistence paid off!

"We did. Yes! Coneflowers can grow really tall!" Molly sat up straighter, pleased that Shannon remembered something about flowers, because she absolutely never took an interest in the shop's contents, just the profit and loss numbers.

"He did seem to appreciate the plant," Shannon replied. Molly heard the boredom in Shannon's voice. She lined up the earring with the lilac bush in her backyard now.

"I'm so glad your boss liked it. That's wonderful. But the thing is, I didn't find the earring in the shop." Mic drop. Molly leaned back in her chair, smugly.

"Well, where did you find it? In the parking lot?" Shannon was growing annoyed, mic drop not even acknowledged.

"No. I found it on the trail. On the Buckeye Trail behind the shop."

"Oh. Well, that's odd." Shannon's tone of voice

changed and might have even faltered. "I don't know why you'd find it there."

"Did you go on a hike Thursday before you visited the shop?" Molly sprinted through her prepared question.

"Whyever would I go on a hike in the middle of the workday?" Shannon's voice turned heated. "I'd like you to return my earring and stop with the interrogation. I'll be by after I'm done working for the day tomorrow. You can leave it at the checkout desk, and I'll just get it from the high school cashier." Shannon's anger deflated Molly's enthusiasm about continuing the conversation and keep prodding. Her cousin always used the wrong jargon. All the shop staff called the area where they checked out customers "the counter," not the checkout desk. And Molly was sure Shannon didn't know the names of any of their evening staff.

"That's fine. Maybe I'll see you then." They both hung up without saying goodbye.

Molly let out a long breath and let her head rest on the chair cushion. That was not how she'd wanted the conversation to go.

This rogue rose-gold earring had to be connected to Trevor—Molly knew it. How would it get on the trail if Shannon wasn't on it herself? Her cousin had admitted it went missing the same day that Trevor did. May seemed to think that Shannon couldn't be believed to say anything truthful, and Molly would not disagree. Was she lying? Plus, Shannon hadn't said a word about Trevor yet, hadn't even acknowledged that Trevor had anything to do with their garden center business. No one from the shop had talked to her about it yet. And Shannon had never returned her first voicemail that Molly left on Friday afternoon. Was Shannon avoiding the issue? It all just seemed so bizarre. She wished Shannon was a normal person she could just talk to. Molly stood up to put the earring in her bag to bring to work with her the next day.

Later that morning, Molly got an excited text from Archie saying he had a wonderful time on the Buckeye Trail, with some pictures of mushrooms and an extremely large tulip poplar tree. She sent back a smiling face emoji, a mushroom emoji, and a tree emoji. Molly was glad someone was having a good morning and happy that Archie had finally gone on his hike. She told him she hoped he found a great hiking destination in Boston too. Things felt a lot better between them in her mind after these short, friendly exchanges.

* * *

A FEW HOURS LATER, Molly got a phone call from Joe, May's detective husband. She knew something was amiss right away since Joe was not one to call her and they were all planning on having dinner with

Molly and May's parents that evening at their house. In the milliseconds between seeing who was calling, lifting the phone to her ear, and answering the call, Molly's mind raced from images of May in a car accident to one of the kids in the emergency room. Instead, Joe was calling about Trevor. They had found his body in the river. And so daylight was thrown on Trevor's disappearance, just like the daylight that had dappled the trees on the morning she found the missing earring. For the rest of the day, Molly felt like fog had descended over her life.

18

A CONCERNING LETTER AND THEO'S THEORIES

On Monday morning, the first thing Molly did was deposit Shannon's earring in the empty slot of the money drawer in the cash register. She wrote a sticky note about its location and stuck it next to the register, out of the view of customers. After that, she had to dig into her self-control reserves to stop herself from opening the box of keys until May got to the shop.

At the baseball game on Saturday, May had made Molly promise in whispers that she wouldn't open the mysterious box until May arrived. The fog that had covered Sunday afternoon followed her to Monday morning: Trevor's confirmed death made everything feel harder. Sherlock's warm and furry kitty greeting was welcoming as well as a physical reminder to get to work.

Molly busied herself tidying the shop floor for

the first twenty minutes. She did a sloppy inventory for what she'd need for the next Farmer's Market and broke down and ordered a dozen tomato plants that would arrive Thursday. She decided that she'd probably just pot succulents again on Friday morning before the market. Molly split up a few succulent cuttings that would be ready in a few weeks. She shifted around some pots of hibiscus in the backyard. Molly was downright antsy and couldn't seem to settle on a single task.

Upon Theo's arrival, he called out his normal "Good morning" as the bell on the door chimed and the door closed behind him. Molly knew he hung his hoodie on the coat rack in the backroom without looking. She jogged wordlessly from the greenhouse area where she was dead-heading petunias to the staff area and caught sight of him turning away from the coat rack on the wooden panels.

They made eye contact, and he simply said, "I heard about Trevor."

"I don't know why I didn't text you." Molly looked at the floor.

"I could have texted you too. It's just ... really hard news. Felt like we needed to be together to talk about it."

"It seemed too big to text," Molly agreed.

"He seemed like such a solid guy, funny, knew what he wanted to do." Molly nodded, frowning, near tears. Theo continued, "Hopefully, we can do something nice for his parents or something. Send some enormous living flower arrangement for the funeral."

"You're right." Molly smiled at her friend. "We can always make things feel a little better with flowers, for sure."

"So, ah, how long have you been here?" Theo asked, changing the subject dramatically, and held up a white envelope. "There was an envelope taped to the door with your name on it. Was it there when you got here?"

"Well, that's unusual. No. It definitely wasn't there earlier," Molly said, taking the envelope. She turned it over in her hands, studying the folded paper. "No return address, no stamp. Just my name, and not even my last name."

"Maybe a sales flyer?"

"Addressed right to me? Only my first name typed out?" Molly asked.

"Well, open it. Let's see what it is."

"What if it's anthrax or something?" Molly asked, thinking of the white spores sent through the mail that killed five people in 2001 shortly after the September 11 bombings.

"The Post Office delivered that. This definitely was personally delivered. It had that blue painter's tape on it," Theo countered.

"Which is even weirder," Molly said. Theo folded his arms and gave her a look that she'd seen May give to Noah when he was being ridiculous. Apparently, Theo had been paying attention.

"Okay, okay," she conceded. Molly used her thumbnail to tear the envelope open across the top and removed the contents.

"A single piece of paper, also typed, no signature," Molly narrated. "And, um, oh my." Her voice suddenly became much more high-pitched than she had recalled it being any time in the recent past.

"What? What is it?" Theo took a step to stand next to her and read over Molly's shoulder as she kept reading aloud.

"Addressed to me, Molly. 'Stop playing detective and poking around in business that is not your own. Leave Trevor alone. Don't regret your actions.'" She paused, letting the words sink in. Theo seemed to do the same. When she spoke again, her voice wasn't shaking as much as she expected. "It rhymes and is quite threatening in just three lines." Molly heard herself say the words. They felt so much calmer than she felt.

"Yeah, yeah. Whoa. 'Don't regret your actions?' I mean, what does that even mean? What's this person going to do to make you regret your actions?" Theo asked, panic in his voice. Then he added, "Real creepy."

"Super creepy." Molly turned to look at Theo, panic still not touching her own voice, but her heart rate was rising. "You didn't see anyone when you got here? No one was leaving the parking lot or anything?"

"No one," he confirmed, shaking his head.

Sherlock hopped up onto the stainless steel worktable, making them both jump. Neither had noticed the feline enter the room.

"Oh, Sherlock," Molly said, stroking the black-and-white cat, who instantly started purring and basked in the affection. She rubbed her face against his soft fur. "You always seem to know when something is wrong." Her heart rate dropped a bit with the kitty to cuddle.

"This is really wrong. I think we should call the police again," Theo said with Claudia-like decisiveness.

"But is that leaving Trevor alone? Will the person who wrote this know? I don't want to do something that will make them do something worse than a note," Molly said, her mind reeling.

"Molly, the person who left you this letter is probably the person who killed Trevor!" Theo said, his voice rising uncharacteristically. He pointed his finger for emphasis. "There could be fingerprints or other clues. We need to hand it over to the detectives. They could find Trevor's killer with this."

"Okay. Yeah, you're probably right," she said, both heart rate and breathing quickening again. "I'm freaking out that the killer is reaching out to me, directly to me." Sherlock continued to rub against her hand when she stopped stroking his ears.

"You must be getting close. He doesn't like that you're digging around."

"He?" She paused. "You're right. I think it's probably a guy. I didn't tell you, but Claudia and I went to the bridge to get a look for ourselves yesterday morning." Theo acted surprised but then seemed to expect the early morning excursion. She described the blood they'd found on the damaged parts of the bridge and that they'd seen Brooks there so early in the morning. Her storytelling helped her blood pressure go down, but her worry increased. "So I think it's a guy. Trevor was tall and would probably be difficult to throw around. I really think that the higher blood stains were probably where his head contacted the bridge supports. Ugh. So disturbing to think about." Theo nodded and screwed up his face. "So, like you said, *he* doesn't like that I'm digging around."

"And you need to tell the police about it." Theo pretended to finish her thought.

"But how did he know I was digging around?" Molly didn't respond to Theo's prodding. "Claudia and I didn't tell very many people we were going to the bridge yesterday. We didn't see anyone but Brooks there."

"So Brooks sent the note?" Theo asked. "That seems really unlikely. He's the one that found the broken bridge, called the police, and sprinted here as fast as he could to meet them. He's just as bothered and invested in this stuff with Trevor as we are."

"Right. That's exactly what Claudia and I thought."

"So someone else saw you? Did you park the van right outside the trailhead or something?" he asked.

"No, Claudia thought of that. I drove Scott's car, and we both parked at the hiking shop."

"So maybe Brooks told someone else? I wonder if Claudia or Brooks himself also got a note? You should ask Claudia. Right after you call the police." With that, he folded his arms across his chest to indicate that the discussion was over.

19

PHONE CALLS AND COUNTED KEYS

A police detective scheduled a time for Molly to visit the precinct later that day, at 2:30 p.m., to deliver the note and discuss the case. The friendly woman who answered the phone said that a uniformed officer in a police cruiser would park in their lot until then. Both Molly and Theo felt a lot better. However, Molly wasn't sure what it meant to discuss the case. Would she and Claudia get in trouble for crossing the police tape? Should she tell them about their excursion into the woods early in the morning? It seemed that those actions were the cause of the threatening note.

Molly called Scott to tell him what had happened. Scott had a job in the city but worked from home one or two days a week. He was a web programmer for a cybersecurity firm and loved the challenge of writing code. Physical security was not in his wheelhouse, so he was very glad to hear that a police car would be parked in front of the garden center, watching over his wife. He was shaken and concerned.

"I don't like this. I don't like this at all," Scott repeated a few times. "How did he know you were at the bridge?" Molly had no answer for that question.

After getting off the phone with Scott, she also called Claudia.

"Are you for real? I can't believe what you're saying!" Claudia demanded. "Text me a picture of the note. This is beyond creepy." Claudia reported she had not received a letter herself. However, Claudia worked at the history museum, also in the city. The museum was enormous and did not have just one door where you could tape a letter addressed to Claudia. She had her own cubicle, but she rarely sat there. Claudia said she'd look around and report back later that day. She ordered Molly to do the same after her visit with the detective. They decided together that they would come clean about their early morning visit to the bridge.

Soon after these calls were placed, May walked in. She had not heard any of the latest developments but had just dropped off her kids at her in-laws for their first day of summer break child care. Her mind was entirely elsewhere.

"Let's look in that key box, succulent sleuth," she called to Molly, a huge smile on her face. May said nothing else, not even a hello. At this, Molly just started laughing. She couldn't stop herself. Somehow, May had heard about the ridiculous nickname from either Claudia or Scott. And Molly had completely forgotten the exciting box of keys that had been on her mind when she arrived in the morning. It was Theo's surprised face that put her over the edge, laughing uncontrollably.

"Oh, we have a lot to fill you in on," Theo told May and clapped both hands on the counter. Molly let Theo do all the talking and show off the letter. She continued to giggle, mostly because she was so uncomfortable and hardly knew what else to do. May put her arms around Molly before Theo was done explaining the note and the three calls. Molly was happy for the physical support.

"I just can't believe this is happening." May echoed everyone's concern. "First, a hiker from out of town is killed on the trail, and now the killer is sending you an ultimatum."

"You know, that really means that the killer is local. He didn't move on," Theo mused.

Molly, May, and Theo watched as a police officer parked outside their door, directly in front of the shop. He got out a laptop computer and typed something before he exited the vehicle.

"Hi, folks," the officer said as the front bell jingled above his head. "I understand a threatening letter was taped to the front door? Can you show me where?" The policeman was older than Molly and had kind eyes.

"I'll show you where I found it," Theo said, and stepped outside. Molly and May watched the men point and make hand motions on the other side of the front door. The officer took some pictures and returned to his car.

Shop patrons came in, wondering if the shop had been robbed because of the police car out front. Nearly everyone asked why a police officer was in the parking lot. Molly repeated over and over the lie that it was just part of the investigation. All the shoppers had heard about Trevor's disappearance and the more recent news of his death.

Mr. Davidson came in for more birdseed. His grumpy demeanor was unchanged, despite the good news that the squirrels were leaving the bird feeder alone after he'd installed his new purchases. Even if he wasn't happy, Molly felt good that her advice had helped a customer.

Before lunch, the shop was empty. The mood of the morning had turned less dire with the public security detail—certainly not a private security detail—and the rhythm of helping and checking out customers.

"Well, I'm ready to dig into that key box," May announced.

Theo rounded on her before Molly said anything. "I still have no idea what you mean about a key box. That's the first thing you said this morning."

"Oh, didn't Molly tell you?" May asked, surprised. "I've been dying to get a better look at all of them." She relayed how Molly found the box of keys under the shelf and they both wanted to inspect them but had to leave after the Farmer's Market. Theo followed her into the storage room, and they returned with the heavy cigar box.

The three gathered around the front counter and May flipped the box top open with as much flourish as she could.

"That really is a lot of keys," Theo said, shaking his head. "What were they doing hiding under a shelf?"

"I think we need to count them, sort them out," May said. "I've been thinking about this all weekend."

"You sure have," Molly laughed. It felt good to laugh because something was funny, not because a killer had threatened her.

They sorted the keys into different colors and ages, laying them all out at right angles to each other on the counter. The metal pieces took up nearly the entire counter space. Sherlock had to be shooed away multiple times: he clearly thought that the somewhat tarnished shiny objects that his humans were playing with were toys for him too.

In the end, there were fifty-three keys in total. Six

were definitely car keys because they had carmaker's emblems. One really looked like the key to the back door. Four keys were old skeleton keys. One was broken, perhaps snipped with bolt cutters. Another was painted entirely black and had chips of paint scraped off. Many keys just looked like normal keys to a house—but why so many houses? Some were larger, thicker keys that might pair with a deadbolt lock to a metal door to a business or an office building. And ten were small keys that might secure a locker or a padlock. There were just so many.

Theo had wandered off to help a customer with two small children load birdseed into her trunk. Sherlock was curled up in the display window in a beam of sunshine. The twins were left staring at the keys together, wondering how they came to the garden center.

"So are these just all the keys that Grandpa ever owned?" May asked, elbows on the counter, her head propped up on her hands.

"Or maybe Grandma? Or both?" Molly added. She paused as she adjusted the keys so they were as straight as possible in their rows. May saw what she was doing and did some adjusting as well. "But why are they here? Why wasn't this box at their house?"

"And"—May shifted her stance and raised a pointer finger—"why was it hidden?"

"Well, maybe it was just lost? Maybe misplaced?

Maybe they didn't intentionally hide it under the shelf?"

"I suppose not. There are just so many things I wish we could have asked Grandma and Grandpa. So much was lost when they passed," May lamented. The twins sighed at the same time, in their frequent twin fashion, and stared at the keys in silence for a moment.

"This one isn't a key," Molly said, pulling out a bit of wire that was left in the box. It had been stuck between the paper cover and the side of the box. "It's practically a paper clip."

"Well, if it's in here, maybe they used it as a key to something, right?"

"Maybe it's a lockpick?" Molly suggested. One end of the wire was bent into a right angle. That part was less than a quarter of an inch long and looked worn. The other end of the wire had a twist to it, not quite turned into a circle, but almost. Perhaps, Molly thought, that end was meant to hang on a hook.

"Well, I'm going to try the keys in each of the doors here. There aren't that many," May declared. With that, she selected several keys and made her way to the back room.

20

SORTED POTS AND A KNOTTED SECRET

"Not that many?" Molly mumbled to herself. May was kidding herself: there were *so many* keys. Nevertheless, she agreed with May that the logical next step was to try them in the locks at the shop. Before Molly could collect some keys herself to try on a door, she got a text from Archie: "Leaving town in a bit. Thanks for everything! Will get back to you on articles—and some Boston hiking trails!!"

Molly smiled and was struck by some hiking inspiration. She wrote back, "It was great meeting you in person too! You should hike around Walden Pond. It's close to Boston! Send me pics!!" She was glad she had gotten to meet her editor and spend time with him, even if he was so much more chatty than he was in email. She had always wanted to visit Walden, where the great thinker Henry David

Thoreau wrote and grew his own plants so long ago. And she was glad to know that Archie didn't have anything to do with Trevor's death.

With that somewhat happy thought, Molly selected a few of the heavier keys and went to the front door, the lock that was right in front of her. She waved to the policeman, who glanced at her, and tried each key. Not a single one fit. She went back to the counter, collected some of the medium keys that looked like they belonged to houses, and returned to the door. Theo came back in from loading the customer's trunk. None of the medium keys fit either.

May returned from the back room, triumphant, holding a key aloft as if she were the winner of a chariot race. "This key opens the door to the backyard! You were right!"

"Alright! We've got one!" Theo pumped his fist in shared celebration.

"But none of these others fit anything. I think we need to be more organized about this," May said. "I'm sorting them into pots by size to try in the locks as a group." With that, she collected some seedling pots and put all the house key lookalikes in one. Another pot received the ten small keys, another one the larger keys, and so forth.

"Which pot do I get?" Theo asked.

"How about you keep trying keys in the front door? I'll look around for other locks that we've overlooked," Molly told him. Theo took the pot with the heavy keys wordlessly and went directly to the front door with a determined look on his face.

She wandered around the shop floor and shoppable greenhouse. As expected, no keys were required in these areas. Their single public bathroom had a lock, but they opened it with a screwdriver if needed. No key was required on that door. Molly headed into the back of the shop, the staff area, and took an inventory of other locks. The money box that they used at the Farmer's Market had a key, but it was just kept in the box itself, which was never locked. She discovered that the stockroom had a lock she'd never noticed, as did the breaker box. That bathroom also had the not-so-secure pop button lock that didn't use a key, only a screwdriver in an emergency.

As Molly's eyes crept over every corner of their storage and work areas, her mind wandered. She had been threatened today by a person who had taken another person's life. That had not quite settled in her mind yet. She wanted nothing more to do with trying to track down this person, she decided. It wasn't Archie, and it wasn't Shannon—probably? She wasn't a detective, and she did not want to push this person into doing anything like what he did to Trevor. She'd talk to the police and make sure they knew what she did, but she'd leave it be after that. Case closed.

Decision made, Molly pursed her lips and

nodded. Her eyes stopped on the wooden paneling on the back wall of the workroom. There was one panel that her eyes always tripped over. It had a big knot and looked like it had been installed after the rest of the wall because it was ever-so-slightly lighter brown wood. No lock here, but she wanted a closer look anyway. She ran her fingers over the divide between the wood panel next to it and the lighter wood. She stuck her fingernail into the knot and knew exactly where to look next.

"May! Theo!" Molly hollered, without thinking about who else might be in the shop. She dashed back to the front counter and slid her eyes over all the keys. She found the one she needed.

May came running from the back room with her pot of keys, and Theo emerged from the greenhouse —he had given up on the front door, apparently.

"Did a key fit? What did you find?" May asked breathlessly.

"This one, this little piece of wire. I think it's really a key! A key to a secret panel. In the workroom." Molly stumbled over her words, too excited to say exactly what she meant. Both May and Theo made excited exclamations that Molly didn't hear. They followed Molly to the staff area.

Molly motioned toward the wooden panel. "I've always wondered what was up with this panel. Have you guys?" Theo nodded, but May made a questioning look, knitting her eyebrows together. "Well, it's a different color, right? And this knot ..." She rubbed her hand over the knot and pointed at a tiny slit in the wood hidden by the knot. She slid the right-angle end of the wire into the slit and turned. She was right! It was the exact size. She expected a click or some sort of physical change, but nothing happened.

"Well ..." Molly breathed. What else did she need to do?

"Pull!" Theo encouraged her.

"Oh. Right," Molly said as she pulled on the wire.

The entire panel fell off the wall and clattered onto the floor. A cloud of dust made Molly sneeze, Theo cough, and May lean back in disgust. The musty smell of a closed-up space wafted out of the cabinet. For a few seconds, the dust hid their view of the contents of this newly revealed secret cabinet.

21

A SECRET CABINET AND THE POLICE STATION

Once the dust had literally cleared, Theo cheered. "This is so cool! How did we never know it was here?"

At the same time, May said, "So what's in it?"

Molly brushed away some dust and spiderwebs and then wiped her hand on her pants. Thankfully, the spiders weren't actually behind the panel right then. "Books?" she said as she picked up one of four leather-bound books tucked in the panel.

May pushed around Molly and announced, "There's also another cigar box." She picked it up and continued, "Not as heavy, so certainly not full of keys."

Molly opened the book she was holding and found her Grandmother's handwriting. Before she'd barely registered that it was a journal with a date listed at the top of the page she had turned to, May exclaimed, "Guys, there's a lot of money in here!"

"Money?" Theo and Molly said together. All three of them laughed.

"Hey, I finally jinxed a twin!" Theo said with a smile. "But seriously, how much money?" he asked, looking over May's shoulder.

"Has it deteriorated since it's been hiding in a wall for years?" Molly asked.

In addition to the cigar box, there were also multiple envelopes that had yellowed with age. Some envelopes were less yellowed than others. Each of them took an envelope to inspect.

"There are lots of bills in this one, not organized at all, though," Molly reported about her envelope. She saw one-, five-, ten-, and twenty-dollar bills, but not any larger than that. They were not in any order and turned every which way. A few were folded in half together and perpendicular to the majority of the bills.

"This one too," Theo agreed, thumbing through the envelope he was holding.

"So a lot of money, but who knows how much? I guess we have to organize the envelopes just like the keys," May said with a wide smile.

"I just can't believe—" Molly started to say, but the front door chime interrupted her. The three of them looked in the direction of the sales floor.

"I'll get it. You guys organize and count," Molly

volunteered. The others agreed without looking up, and she pushed away from the table. When Molly looked over her shoulder as she exited the staff area, May had already pulled her long hair back into a ponytail and was sorting bills into piles according to denomination. Theo was extracting and unfolding bills from the ten or so envelopes in the cigar box as well as more that were loose in the cabinet. Molly felt a thrill of excitement at finding an unknown amount of hidden cash, but what she wanted most was to dig into her grandmother's handwritten notebooks.

The next couple of hours were busy helping customers and eating lunch in the lulls. Glenn came over from the hiking shop to discuss the presence of yet another police car in their parking lot, as well as the news that Trevor had died. He was worried about the reputation of the Buckeye Trail. He said, "We've got such an involved Buckeye Trail Association. Trail Towns, organized events. It's a good trail. Not dangerous." He repeated this last part two more times during their conversation, and Molly could do nothing but agree.

After Glenn left, Molly spent a lot of time helping a customer find the perfect Harry Lauder's Walking Stick shrub for an upcoming gift for her mother. The shrub had twisted, woody branches that Molly often enjoyed describing as "charismatic" to gardeners who leaned more toward the rarer variety of plants.

May had finished sorting the money, but the

sheer amount of individual bills was a lot to actually count and keep track of. May had stacks and stacks of one-dollar bills in piles of ten. Theo thought they just needed to bring it to a bank to use one of their counting machines. Neither of the twins felt right about it leaving the Patty's Plant Place property yet. No one was sure when to tell Shannon about the find.

At 2:15 p.m., Molly left for the police station, followed by the officer in the police car. Her time at the station felt short. She spoke with a bespectacled detective by the name of Eskar, who looked familiar and too young for the job. He might have been one of the officers they'd seen inspecting the trail and putting up the police tape. She handed over the envelope with her threatening note, which she had kept in a single-use zip top plastic bag most of the day. That was Theo's idea. He was very concerned about keeping the evidence unaltered. Detective Eskar ushered her to a rather beige conference room with very hard, heavy, wooden furniture, where he recorded their conversation and took copious notes. Molly had expected to see two-way mirrors but was let down. He barely looked at her as she spoke. She confessed that she and Claudia had breached the police tape and visited the bridge early in the morning hours the day before. She said that they saw a runner but did not give Brooks' name at first. That wasn't something that Claudia and Molly had talked about, and she felt like it was throwing Brooks under the bus if she told the detective who he was. She still didn't know why he was there, why he ran away from them, or if he was connected to the bridge in some other way. The detective asked if she'd recognized Brooks, and Molly, not wanting to lie at the police station, admitted he was the one who called the police in the first place. Eskar just nodded at this revelation and didn't seem concerned. She asked more than once about the blood that seemed to have been cleaned up on the bridge. The detective just made noncommittal comments about not having enough records in the database, but Molly believed he wasn't telling her everything.

She also told Detective Eskar that she was very concerned about the threat and didn't know how to react. He said, "These sorts of things usually are just threats. Murders like this one are rarely planned. The perpetrator likely acted in the moment and did not mean to kill the young man."

"That makes sense," Molly said.

"He or she is very scared right now and is terrified of being caught," the detective continued. "The fact that the letter was typed means the person is being careful and doesn't really want to confront you. We know you've been threatened and will add both your workplace and home to multiple uniformed officers' routes for the next several days. I've given you my card and expect that you will call me directly and immediately if anything else like this happens. In the meantime, don't interact with people you don't know in private situations. Stay in public places, and lock your doors at night. Do you have a security alarm at your home?"

"Erm, no, we don't," Molly answered. His directions were putting her on edge as much as the note had.

"Well, make sure you program my number into your phone, as well as 911. Keep it on you. And stay away from the crime scene from now on."

So much for not being involved, Molly thought.

22

THE RUNNER AND A FLOWER ARRANGEMENT FOR A FUNERAL

Molly returned to the shop to find that May had already left. She had long since put all the keys back in the storage room in their newly sorted key pots. Molly had only another hour or so until her shift was supposed to end. She didn't think she had the time or energy to try more keys on more locks without her twin sister. She filled Theo in on her interview with the detective and thought she'd call both Claudia and May on her way home to tell them the details.

It was busier in the afternoon than in the morning at the garden center. She was glad Aiden had showed up a bit earlier than he normally did, probably because he, like May's kids, was in his first week of summer vacation.

Theo came and hovered over Molly, who was kneeling on the floor as she restocked and organized the display of gardening kneelers. He spoke in a hushed voice, bending down so his face was closer to hers: "Isn't that the runner? The guy who discovered the broken bridge, the same person you saw yesterday morning really early? You know, when you and Claudia were there?"

"Brooks? Where? I need to talk to him!" Molly stood, her head swiveling wildly to catch a glimpse of the man. She wasn't sure how he was involved with all of this, but she wanted to know. But would confronting him mean she wasn't leaving the issue alone like the killer wanted her to? Was he really the killer? Would this also go against the detective's instructions of being alone with someone she didn't know?

"Outside. He just parked his blue car by the trail and is stretching. Like he's getting ready to go on a run. I guess he's going in the opposite direction." Theo wasn't looking at Molly, but stood with his hands on his hips, his line of sight on the far end of the parking lot. Molly strained to see where he was looking. "He parked behind that big silver van. You probably can't see him anymore."

"Theo, we have to talk to him!" Molly whisper-yelled.

"Yeah, yeah. I can finish what you're doing. He's still there, I think. I haven't seen him head for the trail yet."

"But the letter from this morning! What if the guy is watching the shop or something?"

"Oh, you're right. Yeah. Yeah," Theo said, rubbing the stubble on his chin. He paused for just a beat. "Okay. I'll go talk to him."

"You will?" Relief washed over her, along with gratitude for the loving person Theo was. "Can you ask him why he was there that morning? And ask what he found. And why he ran away from us ..." Before Molly felt like she was quite done listing what she wanted to discuss with Brooks, she saw him emerge from behind the van and take off toward the trail, already running.

"I'll let you know!" Theo said as he left at a sprint out the door behind Brooks. Molly was glad that Theo regularly wore running shoes to work. He was certainly much more fit than she was from playing on the minor league soccer team. She had no chance of catching the runner, but Theo definitely did.

Aiden looked up from behind the counter and made eye contact with her, a questioning look on his face. She shrugged, trying to appear unconcerned. The two customers that were nearby didn't seem to have noticed Theo's sudden exit. Molly watched as he ran across the parking lot. Theo was so much faster than she would have been.

Molly finished her restocking and stood behind the counter with Aiden, who rang up bags of topsoil and mulch for one of their customers. Theo would have offered to help load the purchase, but Aiden did not. The man didn't seem to notice.

Molly didn't even realize that Charlotte arrived for her shift because she was worrying about what was happening with Theo. He had been gone fifteen minutes. How long were they going to talk? Should she call the police for the second time that day? Maybe she should text him. He probably had his phone in his pocket, right? Did she just send Theo off into the woods with a killer who had committed murder on that very trail the week before?

To distract herself, Molly ducked into the staff area and went over the two living flower arrangement orders that May had put on the worktable for her. More succulents, this time with orchids. She'd need to order some orchids. The other order was for a funeral, with nothing specified. She knew she would enjoy the creativity of an open-ended project. Oh, where was Theo? Molly made some sketches for the funeral arrangement with white iris bulbs and white lilies with a small evergreen tree. She always thought evergreens were good in funeral arrangements. Should she add some twigs? Did that remind people too much of death in a morbid way? As she considered this, the front door chimed and Molly jumped. Was it Theo? She looked at her watch. It had been thirty-seven minutes since Theo had raced out the door. She'd normally be leaving for the day in a few minutes.

Molly put down her pencil and turned to leave the workroom. Theo collided with her before she was fully out of the doorway. He was out of breath, sweaty, and smiling.

"You are seriously not going to believe what Brooks just told me! You will never, ever guess. Ever," he told her, eagerly making chopping motions with his hands with each syllable.

"Theo! You were gone so long! I was so worried!" She shoved him, but it was a loving shove, a show of concern. He still smiled and shook his head, waiting for her to guess at his announcement. "Okay. What is it? What did Brooks tell you? I'll never guess."

"Brooks is involved with Shannon," he said, eyes wide.

23

BROOKS AND SHANNON

"Okay. Wait. Shannon? Our Shannon? Our cousin?" Molly asked, dumbfounded.

Theo nodded. "The very one." He smiled even more broadly.

"How do you mean involved? Like romantically? Shannon has been with her fiancé, Kalvin, for years. I don't think they ever plan on getting married. Maybe they aren't that happy? But she has that immense ring. Are you sure? Brooks doesn't really seem like her type." Molly knew she was babbling much more than usual.

"No. Not *romantically*. They're involved *financially*." He drew out the last word. Molly could tell that Theo was loving the misunderstanding and suspense he had built by not telling the whole story right away.

"Okay. Financially. What does that mean?"

"I think we should call May and tell her too," Theo told her, stalling. He pulled up a stool and sat down beside the worktable.

"Theo! Just tell me! You're killing me, not spilling this news." Molly was near yelling with excitement and frustration at her friend.

"Killing you? Too soon, Molly. Too soon." He chuckled.

"You know what I mean. Tell me what's going on with Shannon and Brooks."

"Okay, fine." Theo rolled his eyes, still smiling broadly. "So, Brooks works as a janitor at the building where Shannon's real estate company has their office. I bet you never guessed that!"

"That is a very ... interesting coincidence ..." Molly said. This piece of information needed to settle for a moment.

"His wife died a few years ago of ovarian cancer, one of the tough ones," Theo continued, smile gone. "He has huge medical bills from her treatment, as you can expect."

"Well, that's really sad," Molly said, and blew out a breath. She also moved a stool so she could sit down at the worktable.

"His position as a janitor doesn't pay well, and he's interested in changing careers and becoming a real estate agent." He paused for emphasis and leaned forward. "Like Shannon."

"Oh. Like Shannon," Molly confirmed. "She does always seem to have enough money. Not someone I'd want to emulate, though." She felt some of May's resentment of Shannon in her voice and tried to push it away.

"So, Shannon is helping him pay for real estate classes and gives him a bit of money every week to help pay his wife's medical bills," Theo said, tilting his head. "In return, he does some cleaning at some of the buildings or offices she's selling. But it seems like she's really overpaying for that. She's supporting this guy."

"Wait, wait, wait. Shannon is helping Brooks? Like, genuinely helping? There has to be something more going on." Molly knew that's what May would say. She tried to let her mind see another side of Shannon, a pleasant side. A giving side that understood profits weren't the only thing in the world.

"It doesn't really sound like it. I don't think they are involved romantically at all. Like you said: he's not her type."

"Shannon is supporting Brooks." Molly stared into the middle distance and let this settle in her mind more. She needed to interrogate this idea. It was just so foreign. Her cousin was nearly an enemy in her mind, as well as in the conversations she had with those around her.

"They meet here a lot," Theo continued, without

letting Molly think long enough about how her view of Shannon's character had just flipped.

"Here?"

"Yeah. Brooks runs on the trail here, and Shannon needs to stop here to throw her power around and be rude to May." Theo chuckled a little at his own humor. "She doesn't want people in her real estate firm knowing that she's supporting Brooks, so they needed somewhere to hand off the money. I guess she gives him cash so there's no paper trail, and she doesn't want to leave it in an envelope in her office with his name on it or something." Excited by all these revelations, Theo kept waving his arms around as he spoke.

"That makes sense," Molly said slowly. Hadn't she just said those exact words to Detective Eskar earlier that day?

"Brooks never knew that Shannon had a connection to Patty's Plant Place. He just thought that they were meeting here because he runs on the Buckeye Trail, and he runs here often, it seems. They meet on the trail, not in the parking lot where *we* would see them. So she hikes down the trail, probably not in those high heels, I guess, and meets him at a specific rock or at the bridge or something. I don't know why they change it, but they do. So that's why her earring was on the trail."

"And she's supposed to pick it up later today.

Really soon, probably," Molly said, looking at her watch.

"So when all this stuff with Trevor went down, and he came into the garden center, Shannon told Brooks that she's part owner of the shop. She specifically told him not to talk to us again, especially not you and May. Because she's so secretive about this nice, supportive, money-sharing side of herself," Theo leaned back in his stool, his story concluded, points made, Shannon's heart laid out.

"So that's why he ran from us yesterday morning," Molly concluded.

"Right. That's why," Theo confirmed. Then he added hastily and quickly, as if he had forgotten: "And he made me swear not to tell you any of this."

"What! Theo! You broke your promise instantly!" It shocked Molly that Theo would swear something and then take it back so quickly.

"I sure did. But now I'm going to have you swear that you and May won't tell Shannon. Now we all know that Shannon's secretly a goody-goody; we know who she really is. She's not the monster that May makes her out to be. Seriously, she's probably worried that we see her park and walk down the trail as it is when she's here. She's probably nervous when she's here." He crossed his arms for emphasis. "And feels left out of the twin club." Molly knew that he himself often felt left out of this so-called twin club.

"Well, I can't help that she's not my twin. No one

is going to have the same relationship that I have with May," Molly said in self-defense.

"But she's your only cousin in town. You should try to be nice to her. At least a little," Theo said, and then looked at the floor.

"Well, then, you need to be nice too!" Molly poked Theo in the arm. "But what about his visit to the bridge when Claudia and I were there? What was he doing so early in the morning?"

"Oh, right. So I guess Shannon asked him to go make sure her fake nail wasn't there."

"What! She wears fake nails?" This felt nearly as shocking as Shannon's unexpected and secretive generosity. Molly stared into the middle distance again to let this new revelation sink in. Shannon's nails never seemed fake. They always seemed neat but not flashy like her clothing. Molly looked at her own nails. They were short and often dirt-stained because her hands were frequently in potting soil.

"I guess so," Theo said, dismissing the issue altogether. "Anyway, they met on the bridge last week, and she lost a nail then. As you'd expect, she prefers not to be in the woods as long as it would have taken to really inspect the bridge. She asked Brooks to, and he was of the same mind as you were that your police tape jumping shouldn't be in the middle of the day."

"So, it's not like he was looking for something to do with Trevor. He was helping protect Shannon. She has nothing to do with Trevor. He ran from me and Claudia to protect her." It did all fit together. Molly had just never seen this side of Shannon before.

"So can I call May now?" Theo smiled as he asked the question.

24

REFLECTIONS AND A NEW RECIPE

As Molly drove home, she couldn't bring herself to call either Claudia or May. The day had been too eventful, and she needed some quiet time to be with her thoughts and review what had happened. First, an anonymous murderer told her to leave him alone. That in itself would have made any day extraordinary and unsettling and set the manic mood for the rest of the day. After that, they finally organized and enumerated the keys found under the storage shelf. One key led to a secret cabinet with an unknown amount of cash and a connection to Molly's grandma, whom she missed dearly. Next, she talked with a police detective who told her to be extra careful and that she'd frequently see police cars to protect her. This need to be protected felt scary. And to top it off, her view of Shannon's character had been turned on its head with the revelation that she was helping a person in need. All this on a Monday. What would the rest of the week bring?

To treat herself, Molly stopped at the Scottish Ferret and ordered a chocolate peanut butter milkshake to go. She also got a mint chocolate chip milkshake for Scott. He probably wouldn't be home when she arrived, but he'd be really sad if there was no milkshake for him. The Ferret offered waxed cardboard to-go cups that were compostable, and Molly was glad she had her reusable stainless steel straw in her bag.

As she slurped the sugary chocolate and peanut butter treat while driving slowly through town, Molly asked herself if she was doing the right thing. Was she reacting to this note irrationally? Should she have pressed harder? Should she have taken up the detective's mantle and ignored the criminal? Was she being cowardly by going to the police? Or was she being smart? She didn't settle on any answers before she turned the van into her driveway.

At home, Molly stood in front of the open refrigerator, considering dinner options but not really taking in what was in front of her besides the mint chocolate chip milkshake. She and Scott were trying to practice Meatless Mondays to reduce the carbon footprint of their food, and that meant tonight's dinner needed a bit more thought. She decided May's sharp mind would help her make sense of the day and gave her twin a call before settling on meal preparation.

May wanted to hear everything, and so Molly spent a very long time going over every detail that she remembered about her conversation with the detective and what Theo said about Shannon. May asked just a few questions and made short, understanding interjections where appropriate. She had always been Molly's perfect listener.

"Eskar's one of the good ones," May concluded after Molly's monologue. "The case is in excellent hands with him. I wish you had a security system at your house or at least a doorbell camera. I'd feel better."

"Neither is really going to stop him from coming here," Molly said. "Both would just be a warning when it's too late. But telling you all of it makes me feel a little better, at least. I'm just not sure I did the right thing."

"What else would you have done? Confronted a mystery person? Left a note in reply? Anyway, I don't really know what the note was supposed to accomplish. It's not like you have really special knowledge or actually know who he is. All you did was go on an early morning hike." May was getting worked up.

"Well, I asked some questions of Archie and Shannon," Molly interjected. She had thought a lot more about Trevor than May had. And May had not been the least bit concerned that Shannon was MIA for two days. Molly had done much more than just go on a morning hike. She paced in the kitchen while they talked and occasionally reached up and hit the string on the ceiling fan when she passed it.

"But how would he know you talked to Archie and Shannon?" May asked. "Neither of them would have told Trevor's killer about your conversations."

"Okay, that's true. And speaking of Shannon, what do you think of all this stuff with Brooks?" Molly changed the subject. She was nervous about May's response to this revelation about their cousin's character and wanted to help her sift through it.

"I suppose it's nice to know that she can be nice to *someone*, but she's never been nice to me." May's tone of voice was fierce, unforgiving. Molly could picture her chin squared and her back straight, defensive when she didn't need to be. "Even when we were kids, she always made fun of the clothes I wore and the books I read."

"I know, May. She's always been especially mean to you," Molly whispered, and paused for a beat. "But at least she has some capacity to help people, an inclination of kindness somewhere. It's something."

"It is something," May agreed. The twins finished their call soon after.

Molly also called Claudia to fill her in on the rest of the day's events. Claudia confirmed that she had not received a note herself. She worried about Molly being home alone, but Molly reassured her that she had locked the doors and had programmed Detective Eskar's number into her favorites contacts on her phone.

After the info had been downloaded to her inner circle, Molly felt more relaxed and confident that her decision to go to the police was the right one. Theo had thought so too, after all. Molly went back to considering dinner options and settled on a new pasta and asparagus recipe with a cream sauce that she had been wanting to try. She added vegan bacon that they had in the freezer. Meatless Mondays challenged her creativity but made her feel good that she was helping the planet by eating food that produced fewer greenhouse gas emissions. The kitchen work felt productive and calming after a day filled with worry and doubt. She even made salad dressing from scratch. When she came back into the house from dumping her asparagus stubs and lettuce ends into the compost pile, the meal was nearly ready. Scott came home to a delicious-smelling kitchen and a happy, humming wife. He mentioned he saw a police car turning off their road when he pulled in. Scott hugged Molly for a long time upon his arrival, still holding his lunch bag. Their physical connection helped the rest of Molly's worry seep into the floorboards.

25

AN UNLOCKED SHOP AND A BIG DISCOVERY

Scott had forgotten that he needed to pick up a book that he had on hold at the library just before it closed at 9:00 p.m. It was the last day he could pick it up. Molly remembered vaguely that he had mentioned it a few days before. So Scott rushed out to the library, promising that he'd be back as quickly as he could. Molly said she'd be fine at home by herself and didn't want to leave. She locked all the doors and turned on all the lights on the first floor, plus the porch light. Scott seemed satisfied, and Molly felt smug that she didn't need to be protected quite as fiercely as he thought.

Right after he left, Molly received a text from Charlotte. The high school student was closing the shop for the night but had uncharacteristically forgotten her key. Aiden, who was also there, had not been trusted with a key. Molly told her to just turn on the security alarm, and Molly herself would lock up. She texted Scott about this development, and he called her almost immediately.

"So, should I turn around and pick you up?" Scott asked. "Can you wait till I get home? I'm almost there."

"No, I'll just go do it. It'll be fine."

"I don't think so. I don't want you alone at the shop after this incident with an anonymous letter from a murderer. And the police told you to not be out in public alone. You can't go by yourself."

"That's not what they said at all. They said not to be alone with someone I don't know. He said not to go back to the crime scene. The detective said nothing about being in public alone," Molly reported back, feeling irritated. She did not like this feeling of being a damsel in distress. She was sick of feeling scared all day. She felt like Claudia, ready to just do what needed doing.

"Well, I'll drive you there, even so. Or at least ride along. Safer to not be alone."

Molly sighed, unhappy with Scott feeling like she needed an escort. "How is he even going to know I'm there? It's after the shop is supposed to be closed. I'm not worried. I'll be really quick, and Glenn will probably still be closing up." She waited a beat and added, "I'll be home before you finish unloading the dishwasher. Twenty minutes."

"Wait, what?" Scott said. "How did this turn into

me doing chores and not acting as a stand-in security guard?" Molly could hear his smile over the phone. She smiled to herself too: she often got out of arguments with Scott this way by assigning him something to do. Somehow, it diffused a heated situation. "I don't think so. But I do want my book. I'll get it and then you can drive to the shop in the van and I'll ride with you. I'll read while you drive."

"I really don't think I need an escort. I'll just be driving, mostly. No one drove me home. How about I pick up some of the M&M trail mix for you while I'm there?" She knew the way to this man's heart.

Scott let out a long sigh, and he waited so long to respond that she thought he might have hung up. "So trail mix and chores, huh? Pulling out all the stops. You're not going to let this go, are you? I guess you have a point about driving. You did drive to and from the police station and home." He sighed again. Molly nodded as if he could see her. "And you'll only be there a minute to lock up?"

"Just to lock up and grab the trail mix." She nodded again to the empty living room. "I don't want to leave it unlocked for a long time. If it was just me and May who had the garden center, things would be different. But there's Shannon too. I know we live in a safe town, but I'd feel horrible if something happened."

"Well, I'd feel horrible if something happened to you!"

"Scott, come on. I'm leaving now, and you're not here. It will be fine."

"Leaving now?" Scott sounded panicked but then continued in a calmer voice, "You'll have your phone right with you?"

"I'll hold on to it the whole time. I'll be real quick," she told him. "You get your book, Scotty, and I'll get you some trail mix."

"Be safe. And I'll finish the dishes."

They said their goodbyes, and Molly slipped on a hoodie over her pajama shirt. She considered putting on jeans instead of her lounge shorts but decided no one would see her, anyway. At least she was still wearing a bra.

As she was getting into the delivery van, Molly's phone rang. It was Claudia, and she was hysterical.

"Molly. Molly. Oh, my goodness. Craig. Oh ... ooohhh," she said through tears.

"Claud! Do I need to come to your apartment? I'm headed out now. Take a deep breath. Deep breath. Is Craig okay? Good job. Another breath." Molly paced in the driveway, van door still open, coaching her friend to calm down. She decided she might as well drive and talk.

"I'm getting in the van now. I'm going to stop by the shop, but I can swing by your place first if you want me to."

"Oh. OH! It was Craig. He practically just told me

on the phone." Claudia finally got a full sentence out, but it made little sense to Molly.

"What about Craig? What did he tell you? Did you guys break up? I'm sorry, Claud."

"He taught at Ohio University!" Claudia blabbered and then began crying again. And it struck Molly. Craig had worked at Ohio University? Trevor had gone to Ohio University. Craig said he was working his way up the United States. Ohio University was well south of Hawthorn Heights and certainly north of Florida Tech. The injuries on his hands—were they really from a fight with Trevor, not gardening? He hadn't bought the veggie plants at the farmer's market. Maybe he wasn't actually a gardener. This all flooded into her head in a matter of seconds.

"But. Craig?" Molly considered pulling over. She wasn't on a busy road yet, but this news was big and it shook her. Another bomb dropping today. Could it really be true? She felt herself staring into space, and that wasn't a good thing to do while driving. "Ohio University? He taught math there? What else did he say?"

"Yeah. He worked at the same university where Trevor went to school," Claudia sniffed. "We were just talking on the phone. He's been working so hard on all these math classes and felt like he needed to finish something before we got together tonight. He said something about not needing to get the syllabuses—no, it's syllabi—together so early at Ohio University. And I kind of just reacted like you did. I connected the dots and asked a few questions."

"He knew you connected the dots?"

"Yeah. I didn't let him finish talking. Instead, I asked if he knew the hiker. I don't know why, but I didn't say Trevor's name. Craig got really mad, defensive. He said he didn't know Trevor, but why would he be so mad if he didn't? He said he had to go suddenly. I don't know what he's going to do. I should probably call the police. Yeah, I will right when we get off the phone." Claudia was her normal self, no longer panicked.

"I think you need to leave. Go somewhere where he can't find you." Molly's worry radar was amping up.

"Oh, man. You're right. I mean, he might have killed someone. Am I dating a murderer? And if he's so mad at me, I might be next."

"I don't like how mad he got so suddenly," Molly said, wheels turning in her head.

"Yeah. Okay. Maybe I'll just get some things and head straight to the police station, not even call them. Check into a hotel after." With the decision made, Molly could hear Claudia moving around her apartment to prepare. Claudia was always ready to take action.

"No way you're staying at a hotel. You're staying at

my house." Molly tried to use her decisive-Claudia-voice so Claudia couldn't argue with her.

"Molls, don't you think your house is the first place he'd look? And he knows how snoopy you've been. If he can't find me, seriously, he'll go after you. He's already threatened you, after all. He must be the one who left the note."

26

PROTECTIVE KEYS AND M&M TRAIL MIX

Molly again felt like she might need to pull over. Claudia's statement that Craig might actually try to attack her next hit her hard. She took a deep breath before repeating, "Might go after me?"

"Well, you know I'm a talker. I totally told him how you thought it might have been Shannon or Archie. I told him about our trip to the bridge. He always acted so amused by your detective work but was also really interested in it. Asked questions. I never for a second thought I was telling the person who killed Trevor all about this. I'm so sorry, friend. I think I really put you in danger."

"Claudia, you did not put me in danger. I'm the one who keeps trying to figure it out. It just never felt like I was in danger when I was doing it. I just felt like it needed doing. I didn't even think about how I might be in trouble. But, I mean, you know it's Craig for sure, right?" Molly didn't know what to think. Her brain kept going in circles about Craig's relationship to Trevor. Why would he kill a student who went to his university? What was the motive?

She arrived at the garden center. "Well, I just pulled into the parking lot. I'm going to go lock up. Do you want to stay on the phone?"

"No," Claudia told her. "I'm about done getting some clothes and stuff together. I'm going to head out, too. I'll keep you updated. And, Molly, be careful. He's already threatened you. He killed a man, practically a boy. Who knows what he'll do next?"

"Right. I'll be careful. You too." They said their goodbyes, and Molly sat in the van for a minute, considering all this news. It was Craig. He was too good to be true, after all. Claudia had fallen for the wrong guy yet again.

Molly decided she needed to tell Scott before doing anything else, and probably May. She unbuckled her seatbelt and craned her neck to look around. The parking lot was empty and lit by LED floodlights, as usual at this time of the night. In the plaza next door, no one was at the hiking shop, pharmacy, or the café. Glenn had closed up quickly, apparently. No cars were passing on the street. She locked the van doors but didn't turn off the ignition. It seemed safe enough to just sit there for a minute.

To be quicker, she texted them both in their group text chain:

"I know this is big news. Will call in a min. Locking the shop 1st. Claud says she thinks Craig killed Trevor!! She is going to the police station now and will stay at a hotel. Be right back." That summed it up well. She was sure they'd both text back before she even locked up.

Stowing her phone in her hoodie pocket, Molly looked around again. Still an empty, well-lit parking lot. Still no cars on the street. No one else around. Moths circled the light above the glass door, occasionally resting against the shade and then taking flight again. She turned the van off and adjusted her keys in her fist, keys out so she could punch someone with them just like her high school basketball coach had taught her to do. It had been a long time since she held keys that way, but it had always made her teenage self feel better while walking to her car in a darkened parking lot at night. But this was her own, well-lit parking lot, and she wasn't in high school. She was an adult, at her own place of business that she partially owned, not a jumpy teenager. Yes, she was here alone, but she was here alone almost every day. It was just nighttime. No difference.

Pep talk given and received, Molly got out of the van and looked around nervously. She closed the van door as quietly, slowly, and as softly as she could. She shook her head at herself. Why close the door so softly if no one was there? She made herself walk normally to the glass double doors without rushing, even if she had keys at the ready to punch a killer in the face. Molly tapped in the security code as a car went by. She turned around and watched it pass at a normal speed, her head matching the pace of the car. Everything was fine, even if her heart was racing.

Inside the shop, Molly turned on the lights and inhaled the happy place, letting the scent of flowers and soil calm her worry. Sherlock came trotting up and wound his body around her legs, as usual. She bent down and stroked his head. She took a second deep breath and closed her eyes for a few seconds. Everything really was fine.

Molly noticed that the M&M trail mix stock was low. Instead of grabbing the second-to-last pack for Scott, she went into the back room to grab a few more for the display. It would just take a minute. Of course, that specific box of single-serving snacks was at the bottom of a pile of boxes of other snacks. No wonder someone else hadn't stocked it. And so she had to move the boxes one by one until she uncovered the box of trail mix bags. She made sure she had her phone in her pocket, ready to make a call, if needed. It would take just a few minutes to get to the right box. Molly felt her phone buzz in her pocket but told herself that she would finish moving the boxes before she looked at it. The monotony of bending and moving calmed her nerves further.

As she was triumphantly opening the box of M&M trail mix, the lights went out. All of them. Molly stood up, initially wondering what had happened to the electricity but not feeling alarmed. It wasn't storming. There were no strong winds or lightning. They had gotten the breaker box updated a few years ago, even. There was no reason for the electricity to go out without warning.

But then the front doorbell chimed.

27

IN THE DARK AND SCARED

Molly stood frozen in place, trail mix forgotten, concern for the shop's electricity problem no longer a worry. Her initial garden center customer service instinct was, of course, to call out and say hello to a newly arrived customer, because the front doorbell had just chimed and that's what she always did. But she was in the dark, and she had so many goosebumps that her skin was absolutely tingling. There was no doubt in her mind: it was Craig and he was here for her. The van was a telltale sign she was at the shop. No one else drove it, and he knew that. She'd told him all about it herself at the Farmer's Market.

She could hear someone moving around slowly through the retail space in front of the shop. Her advantage was that she could walk around the shop in the dark—she knew every corner because she was the one who arranged all the displays in all those corners. This was her garden center, her turf.

And then Molly remembered she had her phone in her pocket. It didn't seem like a good idea to actually call Detective Eskar or dial 911. Craig would hear her voice. Maybe if she got to the stockroom door and closed it and locked it, then she could call. They had just discovered that it had a lock that morning, after all. She could still hear him moving around. She thought perhaps he hadn't even been to the shop before and did not know the layout at all. He hadn't gone into the shop when Hannah invited him, right?

Molly moved silently to the stockroom door to close it, but then realized that her mountain of stock snack boxes was in the way. She couldn't close the door, let alone lock it. Now what? Could she scootch the boxes noisily out of the way? Probably not.

Molly dug into her hoodie pocket and pulled out her phone. She made sure it was on vibrate and turned down the brightness to be safe. She did indeed have many excited and concerned texts from both Scott and May. But Molly didn't have the time or mental capacity to read them all, let alone respond coherently. Instead, she replied as quickly as her thumbs would allow: "Call the police. Craig is here. I'm hiding."

And so she hid. There was a space between the wall and a shelf with other, less bulky stock items. She crouched down and hoped that her fast, ragged breathing wouldn't give her away. There were boxes all around her, and without the lights on, she'd just be another blob. What did Craig really want here? Why did he turn off the lights? And had he really cut some wires outside or something? How much would that cost to fix? Her phone buzzed, but she was too scared to move to look at it.

"Molly? I know you're here." Craig finally made himself known, loud and clear.

Molly closed her eyes. She was in the dark as it was, but if she couldn't see anything, she could pretend Craig couldn't either. He was in the dark too, she told herself. And she was in the depths of the shop, in the back of the messy maze of their storage room. He would not make his way to her quickly if he didn't know his way around—unless he could somehow hear her out-of-control heartbeat that felt like the loudest thing in the world. The police were on the way. This had to be okay. She just had to wait a few more minutes.

Opening her eyes suddenly, Molly had an idea. What if she could creep out the back door without Craig knowing—or hearing her? There was a door from the retail floor to the backyard and also one from a hallway in the staff area. She could make it. Didn't she still have her protective keys? Molly searched her hoodie pocket, but it was empty except for her phone. Her shorts didn't have pockets. She must have put them down somewhere. There was a utility knife in this room somewhere, but no one ever put it away in the same place. She'd never find it in the dark. She could hear Craig trip on something and swear loudly. This might be a good time to move. He was distracted and frustrated from being hurt.

Molly ever so slowly stood, silently scraping her back against the wall to be sure she didn't hit a box and knock it over. She just had to make her way around the other boxes without making a noise, turn the corner out of the storage room, and make it down the hallway to the back door. It wasn't that far.

"Where are you, Molly? I just want to talk," Craig yelled. Molly thought that line sounded like one from a thriller novel, and she knew that a killer in the dark never, ever just wanted to talk.

28

A CONFESSION AND A HISSING CAT

Molly didn't let Craig's yelling dissuade her. Her fear kept her moving. She felt trapped and boxed in among the boxes in the storage room. Getting outside would be safer, even if the backyard was poorly lit. She shuffled toward the storage room door, not picking up her feet for fear of tripping on a box or a random product on the floor. May would be happy that Molly had made a mental note to tell all the staff that the storage room really needed to be kept tidier in the future. She felt her flip-flop bump into something and tried to softly kick it out of the way. The quiet noise was both metallic and wooden against the concrete floor. She realized it was Grandpa Will's screwdriver with the wooden handle that she had left beside the shelf when she found the box of keys. She knelt down and felt along the cool concrete for the tool. It would be the perfect weapon. She picked it up and wielded it like a dagger as she continued her slow travel to the door.

"Didn't you get my note? Just leave this issue alone!" Craig yelled. Molly heard both mania and extreme frustration in his voice. Then she heard him trip and swear again, too. She was sure he regretted turning off the lights. She wished she had thought to record what Craig was saying on her phone. This last outburst confirmed he was Trevor's killer. Her anger boiled at the thought of the damage he had inflicted on her store, mingled with his actions to take the young man's life, even if they weren't planned as Detective Eskar had suggested. Molly wanted to yell an angry response, but knowing his violent tendencies kept quiet. She had to put distance between herself and Craig. She also needed to make sure that he didn't get away and that he would go to jail for his actions. Once she was outside, she'd call Detective Eskar directly, out of Craig's earshot. She realized that she should have texted the detective when she sent messages to Scott and May. Too late for that now.

Molly felt the metal storage room door with her toe. She moved her arm and found the door handle. It was cold and her palms were sweaty. She had made it to the entry of the storage room. Slowly, ever so slowly, she peered around the corner of the door: just enough for one eye to see. Craig was definitely still on the sales floor and had not made it behind the counter into the back of the store. She slowly and quietly blew out a breath she'd been holding for who knows how long.

Sherlock was at Molly's feet. She hadn't noticed how or when he arrived out of the shadows. She was glad to know that Craig hadn't somehow harmed the kitty. He put his front paws on her knees, and she bent down to rub his ears. She considered picking him up so he'd leave the shop with her, but that would mean her screwdriver weapon wouldn't be at the ready.

With one last pat on his furry head, she flattened her back against the wall of the short hallway to the back door. Monitoring the entrance to the staff area, she slowly crept down the hallway, not exactly looking where she was going. The space was dimly lit by the half window on the door to the backyard. There weren't any lights on out there, but the moonlight shone through the window of the door. Craig had been quiet for a few minutes, and she was nervous about what he was doing and where he was. She passed the door of the employee bathroom. It felt like a milestone. She was almost there.

Then, a few things happened at once. She was looking behind her as she crept to the back door, and she somehow stepped on Sherlock's tail or foot despite her slow movements. The cat hissed loudly, and she saw him reel back and then horse-trot down the hall toward the sales floor. As he ran away, her phone buzzed in her pocket with a phone call. She ignored it because Craig appeared at the end of the hallway. Was it Sherlock's hiss that alerted him? She'd probably never know.

"There you are! You need to keep quiet, Molly! Trevor is none of your business!" Craig roared before he barreled down the hallway toward her. He didn't notice Sherlock, who was running toward him. Craig kicked Sherlock in his crazy dash, and the cat responded by clawing Craig's exposed leg. Craig bent down to hold his wound, and the cat disappeared in the dark.

Molly turned before Craig had even kicked Sherlock and ran as fast as she could the short distance to the door. Her legs moved faster than she ever thought they could, her stride practically a split, as if she were jumping like a ballerina. A flip-flop flew off in midair, but it hardly registered in her mind. Her vision zeroed in on the dead bolt. The door was locked. Of course Charlotte would have locked it. Could Molly unlock it quickly enough? Muscle memory would kick in, she convinced herself.

And it did. The bolt slid out of the doorjamb with ease and speed. As she turned the doorknob and opened the door, she glanced over her shoulder and saw Craig nearly upon her. Molly opened the door just enough to slip through and flipped her body around it. She was outside, standing on the deck. She pulled hard on the outside doorknob, wishing she could relock it instead of just close the door. Molly then realized her danger. Craig was stronger than she was and could just pull the door open and out of her grasp. She couldn't get away fast enough to hide somewhere else. She held onto the doorknob with all her strength and leaned back, putting her entire weight into it. The door was latched but not locked. Her toes curled, one foot on the wooden decking and one foot still in a flip-flop.

With all the adrenaline coursing through her body, Molly was aware of the loud insect conversations and frog calls going on behind her in the forest. The air was cool but muggy, ready for another late spring rain. She felt sweat prick along her hairline. She threw her head back, trying to see if an obvious answer would come to her in the backyard, but nothing did.

"What are you doing?" Craig yelled on the other side of the door. He tried to pull the door open, as she'd expected. Molly hung onto the doorknob with everything she had. "You need to stop snooping around. Stop talking to the police. What's done is done."

A tug of war began over the door. Craig had unlatched the door and was pulling it into the shop, toward him, and Molly was straining in the opposite direction, trying to close it. She was losing ground but still leaning back. Then she realized she was still holding the screwdriver under her armpit. Should she drop it to gain more control, or use it as she'd intended when she picked it up? She decided that it was a weapon.

29

A USEFUL SCREWDRIVER AND MORE INVOLVEMENT

Molly's feet were already well planted on the deck boards, but she dug in her heels, moved her center of gravity back, and bent her knees slightly. She was ready for a fight. To distract Craig, she started talking for the first time since he'd entered the shop. She hadn't actually said a single thing to the man yet. The police had to be here soon. Hopefully, she could buy some time.

"So what happened? Why are you saying what's done is done?" She tried to keep her voice somewhat friendly and conversational and not as thoroughly panicked and out of breath as she felt. She felt sweat pool in the small of her back.

"You know, of course," Craig said, his pull on the door slackening just a little. "You saw the bridge. We had a fight." He wasn't yelling now, just stating facts. He knew she and Claudia had visited the bridge.

As Craig spoke, Molly quickly took the screwdriver out from under her arm with her right hand and changed the grip so that she was holding it with the metal end pointed down, ready to stab. She still had a firm grip on the doorknob with her left hand. "But why? Why pick a fight with a college kid?" she asked him.

"This really isn't any of your business, Molly. I'm telling you to walk away from what happened. It doesn't affect you at all," he continued in a calmer voice, while still pulling on the door. He seemed to have realized that she had less muscle behind her tugging and looked her in the eyes through the glass. He gave one huge yank on the doorknob. With this, he gained more ground and could open the door enough to push his shoulder and arm around to the outside.

"Trevor was here! He was in our store and on our trail! It has really affected me!" Molly yelled at him. When Craig's arm appeared on her side of the door, Molly saw her chance and hacked at it with the screwdriver in the dark. Her aim wasn't great, but she sliced at him five times and definitely cut into his arm at least three of them. She didn't really count. Craig shrieked in pain and tried to pull his arm back into the building, but Molly kept yanking on her side of the door and he was pinned.

"You didn't even know him!" Craig bellowed, waving his arm around. His hand tried to grab her, but Molly easily dodged.

"Why does that matter? You knew him and you took his life!" Molly yelled back. She tried to stab at him again, but his arm was waving too violently. Her anger gave her strength to keep pulling on the door one-handed, but not enough speed or aim to follow his arm. Molly could see Craig's face through the window, sweaty and panicked. She realized she had tears dripping out of her eyes, not just sweat.

"Stop that! I didn't mean to! I just pushed the kid! Punched him a few times, but he punched me first." Craig's voice was pleading and loud.

"He was a sweet guy, just a kid. He's like fifteen years younger than you! Why would you ever punch him to begin with?" Molly recognized that not only was she trying to keep him talking to stall until the police arrived, but also she really wanted to know what happened. She grabbed his arm and pinned it against the door. She didn't really expect it to work, but it did. Molly put her entire weight into it. Her face was close to Craig's between the glass, and they locked eyes. "Why?" she asked, moving the screwdriver into his view threateningly. She hadn't known that she was capable of this sort of commanding meanness.

Although it was dark, Molly could see that Craig's face had fallen and turned pale. "He said he'd turn me in. I was involved with his girlfriend. That's frowned upon in any university. It's why I left Ohio University."

Shocked, Molly dropped her arm with the screwdriver to her side. Certainly, this "involvement" wasn't financial like Brooks and Shannon's. Craig had been romantically involved with Trevor's girlfriend, the girlfriend who had broken up with him, who he was hiking the Buckeye Trail to forget. Of course Trevor would be mad and engage in a fight with a former professor. As she slackened her hold on the screwdriver, she heard sirens in the distance. Finally! That must be the police coming to apprehend Craig!

The sirens helped her focus and hold on to the screwdriver. However, Craig took the opportunity of her visible weakness to pull harder at the door. Just as she was straightening up, he gave the door another hard yank. Molly lost her grip. And then there wasn't a door between them anymore.

30

A CORNERED ANIMAL AND POLICE CARS

"Did you call the police? Are they coming here? I keep telling you to mind your own business!" Craig's anger had returned, and was scary and animal-like. He loomed over her in the dark, blood dripping down his arm. It was obvious that he didn't know what to do next. He breathed heavily, fists clenched.

Molly looked over her shoulder briefly as she walked slowly backward. Without the nighttime floodlight, the backyard was dark even in the moonlight. The forest surrounding the Buckeye Trail beyond the backyard was even darker. Should she run into the darkness and hide? She still heard the bugs and the frogs. She knew the winding paths and the taller plants that would hide her from view. There was no way she'd win a fight against this man, screwdriver or not. She just needed a few more minutes for the police to get there. She was so close. And so scared.

But then she heard a car door slam close by. It wasn't the police because Molly still heard the sirens a ways off. Then she heard another car, turning loudly, brakes screeching, and then yet another car door. She made eye contact with Craig. What was he going to do? He was breathing hard, head cocked, also listening, and seemed frozen in indecision.

"BACK HERE!" Molly yelled as loudly as she could. "We're in the backyard!"

"MOLLY!" It was Scott. Of course he wouldn't just call the police and stay at home doing dishes. She would have done the same thing. Her heart soared with love for the man.

"Molls!" And Claudia was here too. She heard more cars. Was it the police without sirens?

Craig's eyes darted everywhere, panicked. He looked like a cornered wild animal. He obviously didn't know what to do. Neither did Molly. But she knew she had to keep him here—and also not get killed herself. Before Claudia finished calling to Molly, Craig tried to duck around her. Molly thought he was making for the woods to hide as she had considered doing just a moment ago. She spread both her arms and legs wide. She moved left and right, trying to block him like a basketball player. He also shuffled left and right. They danced like this for a moment, and then Molly had an idea.

It was the time to be a football player, not a basketball player. So Molly jumped at him, dropping her screwdriver and trying to tackle him. But instead of tackling Craig, she just gave him a great big bear hug with her arms and legs, her body hanging off his. She had never played football, after all. He was so tall that she hung several inches off the ground. He pushed at her stomach, trying to get her off. He hit at her back with his fists. She hung on as hard as she could, locking her hands around her wrists and hooking one foot around the other ankle. They were both yelling. He turned around and smashed her into the building, and all the air in her lungs came out, but somehow she still hung on. This all happened in just the span of a few minutes. She knew she could hang on for another minute. Enough time for Scott and Claudia to get through the building.

And then Scott and May and Theo and Vivian, Theo's future fiancée, were all there. They were pulling Craig away from her. She fell hard on the decking. Claudia was crying and cradling Molly's hand and her head. Once May saw that Scott, Theo, and Vivian had hold of Craig, she held Molly's other hand, asking where she was hurt. Craig was screaming and kicking. Scott, Theo, and Vivian had pinned him against the building.

"You're not getting away, man!" Theo yelled at him. "The police are on their way."

"It was an accident!" Craig yelled back, spitting with emotion and fear. He thrashed against them.

Molly stood up, and so did May and Claudia. Molly made eye contact with Claudia. Then her friend turned to Craig.

"It doesn't matter if it was an accident. You killed a man," Claudia yelled, tears rolling down her face. "If it was an accident, why didn't you call the police? Did you even try to help him? You knew he fell into the water and did nothing!"

Molly picked the screwdriver up off the deck and stepped toward Craig. She knew he would think she was trying to intimidate him, but really she didn't want to lose her grandpa's screwdriver. Now it meant even more to her. As she looked up, he went limp and started crying too. He had given up. They outnumbered him, and he knew he wouldn't be able to fight off six people.

Claudia was still crying. "You're horrible," she said simply, and followed May into the store. The police had arrived: multiple cars with flashing lights had pulled into the parking lot. They would have a hard time navigating through the dark store, but May and Claudia could show them the way.

Molly's back hurt, but the thrill of apprehending a killer on her own turf was worth it.

31

A COMMUNITY BAND CONCERT AND MORE TO COME

Almost a week later, Molly lay on her back on a blanket in the grass, hands tucked behind her head. She looked up at the clouds as they floated lazily across the sky and elm leaves swayed above her. It was such a lovely evening, even if it hurt a little to lie on her back. She was still on prescribed extra-strength anti-inflammatories, but the bruises on her back were fading.

"Want a refill, Molly?" Scott asked, holding up a bottle of red wine. It was already down by two-thirds.

"Maybe after they start. I don't want to be drunk before the performance," she replied with a chuckle.

"Well, I'll take some more," Joe laughed. "Why aren't you offering wine to everyone, Scott?" He held up his stemless wine glass.

"No one else here has an injured back, Detective. Nevertheless, you could do with some more wine too," Scott quipped back and poured wine into his brother-in-law's glass.

It was the Saturday evening following Molly's run-in with Craig at Patty's Plant Place. Molly, Scott, May, Joe, and Theo were all lounging on blankets in the Hawthorn Heights community park, eating a snack-dinner of cheese, crackers, lunchmeat, and pickled veggies. Hannah, Noah, and Vivian were running around the blankets and throwing balls back and forth to each other while everyone else lounged and munched. The community band concert was set to start in less than ten minutes. Claudia was playing the second clarinet. It had been a hard week for her, but preparing for the concert had been a productive distraction.

"I need a break, kiddos," Vivian said as she collapsed on the blanket next to Molly, winded and sweaty. "I haven't seen all of you since that crazy night on Monday. How's your back, Molly?"

Molly sat up and answered: "Oh, it's healing. All those X-rays that night in the ER did seem a bit dramatic. Nothing is broken."

"That's good. I can see by the way you're moving that it's still tender. I'm worried about you having some PTSD, though, after getting into such a physical altercation at work." Vivian looked at Molly seriously. Her expertise as a psychologist was showing. Scott nodded in agreement.

"Oh. Well, yeah," Molly mumbled, thinking

about the question. "The electricity just got turned back on today, so it's been a pretty unusual week. Just accepting cash and checks and limiting hours to when the sun was up and all." She paused, considering. All eyes were on her now. She looked at her friends and family. "Honestly, Craig can't steal Patty's Plant Place from me. It's my happy place. I haven't felt scared in the backyard or worried that something like that would happen again. I think my brain knows that I did a good thing during that fight. I stood up to a bully, and all of us brought a killer to justice. I've been good. Just still sore. And I'm so thankful for all of you." She smiled at Vivian, admiring her braids, as usual.

"I'm really glad to hear that. Glad you're feeling good," Vivian replied.

"But speaking of not talking to anyone since Monday. I really want to hear your side of this engagement story!" Molly said, taking Vivian's left hand and admiring the sparkling ring again.

"Oh, my goodness! What a crazy night that was! So much happened!" Vivian looked sheepish. "It won't be a night any of us forget. Our evening started when Theo asked me to go out to dinner. On a Monday! That's a little odd, right? But we went to that new swanky place in the city, Antonio's. The food was delicious. Then we went to the Botanical Garden."

Theo shifted so that he was next to Vivian and

put his arm around her, smiling. "I really should have done it on the Saturday before, I know."

"Right. I knew something was up when he suggested we go to the Cleveland Botanical Garden on a Monday night, but I played along. They're usually closed on Mondays but it's a special for June, I guess. He's in the know." She elbowed Theo in the ribs jokingly and continued. "It's such a pretty place. He told me about all the different plants and flowers. At the terrace with the pool and fountains, he got down on one knee and asked me to marry him. I cried. It was perfect. The ring is perfect. A bunch of people were there and clapped. It was a beautiful moment."

"I know I said I'd tell you about it, Molly," Theo said. "I promised I'd tell you when it happened."

"You did promise." Molly shoved him and then winced. She shouldn't have moved so quickly because it hurt her back.

"When we were driving back from Cleveland, we got the call from Scott," Theo said, continuing the story. "He told us what was going on, and it just happened that we were less than ten minutes away from the shop. He said that he and May and Claudia were all trying to be there at the same time to outnumber Craig. Scott was worried that the police wouldn't get there in time. I'm really glad we were there when we were. I was just going to text you when I got home. You know, I just wanted to be present with my lady and not tell the entire world right when it happened." He smiled at Vivian.

"He didn't even tell his mom until the next day," Vivian said in a shocked tone. "I told my mom that night after I got home. And my brother and my aunt and my best friend."

"No hard feelings." Molly smiled at them, happy for the couple. "It's okay that you didn't tell me right away. You told me the next day, at least. And I'm so glad that you all came to the garden center when you did. I think he would have run into the woods otherwise and gotten away. I wouldn't have been able to keep him in the backyard for much longer without getting hurt really bad." The others agreed, nodding among themselves.

"I have a big question," Scott said to the group. "This money from Grandma and Grandpa that was hidden in the wall: is it still a secret?"

"Oh, you mean the $33,740 that Grandma had squirrelled away from Grandpa?" May jumped in. "We've been dealing with a crazy store all week. Shannon's upset that we didn't make as much as usual in the second week in June and we have to pay for an electrician. Honestly, I'm hoping that we can buy her out. Just hand over the cash and she'd be out of the business, but we haven't been able to think about how to go about the proposal yet. We probably need to talk to a lawyer. I'm not sure if it's enough money, frankly."

"But we're not sure if that's what Grandma Patty would have wanted," Molly added. "It's a big decision to make. Grandma left the store to the three of us, after all. And we don't know why she hid all the money. It might have been both of them saving together. I've been reading the journals. It's a lot of shop details, not as much personal stuff. I'm hoping that somewhere in there she mentions the money. I haven't found it yet, though."

"Right," May agreed. "There's still information to gather and decisions to be made. We're not doing anything with it right now."

"It's back in the hidey-hole," Theo added. "Much better organized."

"And the keys?" Scott asked.

"We know nothing more," May said quickly. Molly knew she still hadn't said anything to Joe and wanted to change the conversation swiftly "Kids!" she hollered at Hannah and Noah. "Time to sit down and eat. The musicians are about to start!" Subject dropped.

Molly moved so she was sitting closer to Scott and leaned into his shoulder. She was so glad to have the circle of people around her and was ready to enjoy beautiful music performed by her best friend.

NEWSLETTER

Be sure to sign up for Iris March's email newsletter to get Molly's very first mystery, Terra Cotta Theft for free.

A new teen employee. Stolen cash. And a garden center full of suspects. Meet Molly as a teen along with Grandma Patty and Grandpa Will.

ACKNOWLEDGMENTS

Thank you so much to everyone who has helped me get my books off the ground! My husband and son, Nate and Jude, have been my biggest cheerleaders on this book-writing adventure, as well as my amazing mom, Linda. Thank you to everyone in my family for believing in me!

I've learned so much from my friends at Write Publish Sell and my writing group and critique group, the Poison Pens. Thank you to Dallas Woodburn, who helped me tighten up the story. (You're awesome!)

My beta readers are so important to me: they pointed out plot holes and provided wonderful ideas. These brilliant people include Linda, Rhonda, Aunt Peg, Marissa, and Patti.

Thanks to my cousin-in-law Allie for helping me describe Molly's plant work. I am usually a plant killer, but Allie actually works at a garden center and knows her stuff.

Thank you to my friends at the Buckeye Trail Association for their thoughtful responses to all my questions about the Buckeye Trail sections that I have not visited myself but wanted to make up in my head. I want to reiterate again that the section of trail within Hawthorn Heights exists only in my head (and now yours!). To my knowledge, no one has ever died on the Buckeye Trail. It's a good trail, not dangerous, just like Glenn says it is.

Huge appreciation to my editor, Beth. My writing is always better when someone else goes over it with a fine-toothed comb, especially someone who knows grammar better than I do.

And thanks to you, reader!

I appreciate your own investment of time for reading the book! If you enjoyed this story, I would also appreciate a review wherever you bought your copy.

I have another book coming later in 2022, set in the same town but about another runner. There's not a dead hiker but, instead, a mysterious building and the power of teamwork to discover more about the past and bolster individual internal strength. Visit my website www.IrisMarchBooks.com to learn more and subscribe to my email newsletter. And there will be more Succulent Sleuth cozy mysteries to come!

Author's Note

I do not have a green thumb in the slightest, but adore plants. All of Molly's planty knowledge was spoon-fed to me rather than coming from my brain. I have, however, worked in the sustainability field my entire career, and so all the eco-friendly tips sprinkled throughout the book are solid. I encourage you, reader, to do your own part to reduce the impacts of climate change by printing on the second side of the paper, composting, eating less meat, reducing single-use plastic, and using less energy like Molly does. I love to talk about reducing our impact on the Earth, so contact me if you want to chat about the topic (I mean it!).

ABOUT THE AUTHOR

Iris March lives in Ohio with her husband and son on the edge of the Cleveland Metroparks. She has worked in the sustainability field her entire career and has always loved reading. Iris is thrilled to jump into the world of book writing. She enjoys hiking, running, but unfortunately has never had a green thumb like her mother.

An abandoned building. A motivated runner. A Hodgkin's lymphoma cancer survivor.

Connor Jackson has been training for a half marathon for the past six weeks. Katie Brandt has been training to beat cancer for the past 50. When Connor discovers an intriguing secret in a tiny, abandoned building on his running route, Katie finds that the mystery is what she needs to help her get through her three-week stem cell replacement procedure. Together, Conner and Katie must find the strength to achieve their personal goals and, in the meantime, expose the many past lives that the tiny building led.

"We all want to find something amazing - some treasure - in old, abandoned places. That's what we expect."
- Katie Brandt, cancer survivor

Printed in Great Britain
by Amazon